IT STARTED WITH A PIRATE

Coffee, cake and cats: these are a few of Lexie Farrington's favourite things. When she walks into the Thistledean Café in Edinburgh, she's delighted to find all three — including a black cat being held by a very grumpy-looking pirate! Of course, Billy McCreadie isn't really a pirate — he just gives talks about them. But he is in desperate need of a cat-sitter. When Lexie steps in, little does she realise that Billy will be the very man to solve a certain puzzle of her own . . .

KIRSTY FERRY

IT STARTED WITH A PIRATE

Complete and Unabridged

LINFORD
Leicester

First published in Great Britain in 2021
Choc Lit Limited
Surrey

First Linford Edition published 2021
by arrangement with
Choc Lit Limited
Surrey

*A catalogue record for this book is available
from the British Library.*

ISBN 978–1–4448–4760–4

Published by
Ulverscroft Limited
Anstey, Leicestershire

Printed and bound in Great Britain by
TJ Books Ltd., Padstow, Cornwall

This book is printed on acid-free paper

Dedication

To James.
You totally deserved first prize for your
pirate outfit at the Pirates and Princesses
Summer Fayre, all those years ago at
primary school!

Acknowledgements

When I began to think about the story I could invent for Billy, the hero in this, the fourth of my 'Schubert' books, I knew I wanted a pirate theme. In my head, Billy had always been this very attractive man who had drifted a bit until he found a job he was happy in. You may recall he used to be a car salesman in an earlier Schubert book — well, that was no longer the job for him, I'm afraid. My other thought was a highwayman, but I've already written about one and, to be honest, it would be a bit difficult to write about in a modern context — not to mention that Billy might have ended up doing something a little (or a lot!) illegal in that sort of role! So I aimlessly Googled 'Pirate Edinburgh' and came up with an amazing story in the *Edinburgh News* about Victoria Primary School in Newhaven, which had its very own pirate buried in the grounds.

The pirate was unearthed in 2014 when the school was getting some survey work done ahead of a new extension, and scientists have reconstructed his face, as well as working out he was executed and displayed in a gibbet as a deterrent to others.

A bit more research told me that the Sands of Leith were the likeliest place for his execution, and I will be forever thankful to the lovely Joanne Baird from Portobello Book Blog who gave me loads of information about what the area is like now, and also sent me photographs so I could work out exactly where my characters could and couldn't go — you can't get onto the piratical bit of the sands now, but I suspect it still has a strange old atmosphere to it. Joanne also suggested I reword a particular passage, as I had Billy and Lexie somewhere they couldn't possibly be, so a big shout out to Joanne and a huge 'thank you' from me and Schubert!

As I continued to research the story, to my delight I found loads of information from various historical sources that also linked the pirate idea to shipwrecked pirate vessels, the Jacobites (another huge favourite subject area of mine) and the Orkneys. The more I dug into the era, the more I started to see a way for all the pieces to fit together. I also remembered visiting Clovelly in Devon many, many years ago and the thing that struck me there (apart from the donkeys and the massive hill) was the fact that Spanish pirates used to rock up there regularly, and hence many locals were descended from them. My story suddenly all made sense. Therefore, the Tolbooth trials, the report of the shipwreck and the quotes used in this book where piratical punishments were meted out are indeed based on fact, and are all taken from genuine historical records.

Of course, I couldn't have pulled all this together without the support of my fabulous publishers, Choc Lit, and my wonderful editor. Also big thanks to my lovely cover designer, and the amazing Tasting Panel who agreed Schubert's 'tail' could continue with this instalment: Lucie Wheatcroft, Lorna Baker, Joy Bleach, Dimitra Evangelou, Jo Osborne, Jenny Mitchell, Shona Nicolson and Gill Leivers.

And the biggest thanks of all have to go to my family who are forever there for me, with especially big thanks to my son. He had lots of books on pirates when he was small — and it's from reading those with him that the Captain Kidd picture I mention in the book stuck in my head. Although, thinking about it, that's maybe not a great thing to be thankful for!

1

Edinburgh

Lexie

I've always had a fondness for cemeteries. Now, before you run away screaming, I should probably mention that I'm a genealogist. That means it's perfectly acceptable for me to wander around various cemeteries and look at graves and make notes and take photographs.

I have visited cemeteries all over the place; there's always something fascinating to see, like lovingly built monuments and stones etched with all sorts of beautifully worded inscriptions — including one or two inscriptions about people who can't possibly be as good as they're made out to be.

I've found curiously interesting tombs in the Jesmond Old Cemetery in Newcastle-upon-Tyne. A bit further north, the gravestones in Tynemouth

Priory could tell a tale or two. In Wales, a particularly lovely monument behind Rug Chapel had my genealogist's brain clicking into gear. In London, you just can't beat Highgate — I've done the tour there. Twice.

Some people think my cemetery obsession is a bit weird. I know my family does. I live — or rather, my family lives — in Devon. I kind of drift around a bit. I seem to have an inability to stay put anywhere for very long, and today my travels have brought me up to Edinburgh — which is absolutely beautiful, and my latest stopping-off place to who knows where.

Maybe one day I'll settle down . . .

But, until then, I'm happy to roam around cemeteries, and the one I've just visited in Edinburgh is beautiful. Very impressive.

To clarify, I'm not into all the creepy stuff that goes with cemeteries; I don't believe in ghosts, for instance. I absolutely don't. For some reason, it really doesn't bother me that I'm walking around and beneath my feet are the bodies of hundreds of people.

I mean, if a ghost was to come back, why would it want to haunt the place its body got stuffed in the ground? I'm sure I wouldn't. All of that stuff can be explained by tricks of the light and pareidolia — where you see something that looks like a face, so you think it's a face.

It's all hearsay, and until I see a ghost myself — which I won't because they don't exist — I'm happy to dig into the real *actual* lives of people as part of my genealogy role. Far more interesting.

So, I'm not going to fret about ghosts. Once I pop my clogs, there'll be a nice stone somewhere for me that says: *Here lies Lexie Farrington, and her ghost doesn't exist.*

Truth.

What I do believe in and what I like, possibly even more than cemeteries, is coffee, cake and cats. I've just walked into a café in Edinburgh called Thistledean Café, and I do believe there is a combination of all three in here, which is

3

pretty awesome.

I especially like the fact that there is a huge, fat, furry black cat on a purple lead sitting beside the counter, with a bandana around where I think its neck should be — if it was a slimmer cat, that is — and on the other end of the lead is a man with fairly long black hair, tied back in a style that makes him look a bit like a highwaymen or a pirate. He's dressed pretty piratically as well, and I have to say he's looking pretty damn good — a little bit like Bono from U2 did when he rocked that very same hairstyle circa 1987. It was a bit before my time but I've seen the music videos. Can't beat a bit of classic rock. Although, from the expression on this chap's face, it looks like he would rather be anywhere else but here . . .

Billy

'I don't bloody care.' I'm furious, and it doesn't help that my brother is laughing at me. 'Hugo, please, just take Schubert. Please. I can't do this with a sodding cat on a sodding lead.'

'Oh Billy. When can we start calling you Bono, circa 1987?' says Hugo and snorts with laughter again.

'I'm a fecking pirate. I'm not fecking Bono!'

'Bono.'

'Definitely Bono.' That's Maria, Hugo's ex-boss and my best mate Stu's wife. Maria owns the café. Hugo used to work here as assistant manager, until he qualified as a probation officer. God knows what he's doing behind the counter today with that stupid little barista's apron on. '*Joshua Tree* Bono, as I live and breathe.' Maria snorts with laughter as well and I feel my temper rise even higher.

'Look, I love Bono. You know I do,' I say, 'and yes, I may have, very slightly, based this look on him — and Jack Sparrow. From *Pirates of the Caribbean*. You know? A pirate.'

'Bono,' coughs Hugo behind his hand.

5

'But,' I say, choosing to ignore him, 'I can't do a talk to seven million school kids about sodding pirates with bloody Schubert on a bloody lead.' I rake my free hand through my hair — my *piratical* hair — and panic slightly.

'Mow wow,' says Schubert complacently. He's my sister Nessa's cat, and I was too slow to say I couldn't babysit him this week while she's on her holidays. She says she's working from the hotel, but I bet she's not. She works for a private investigator and property mogul, Mr Hogarth, who none of us has ever seen — well, her boyfriend, Ewan, has seen him, but that's only because Ewan is his godson. Ewan is in the film industry and Nessa always seems to get herself invited on his trips away to Hollywood and London. This week, she's in London, but she's due back later tonight, thank God. She should have been back last night, but apparently she decided to, and I quote, 'tag another day on to have dinner with The Boys'. I have no idea who 'The Boys' are, but I'm willing to bet they're famous.

And she's left Schubert, her massive spoiled cat with me.

I am horribly conscious that I have no Plan B for my talk, because she was *supposed to be back yesterday.*

When I'd opened the door to her last week and had seen her there with him and his cat basket, I knew it was already too late.

'Schubert hasn't stayed with you for a while,' she announced. She announced it in a muffled sort of fashion because she had her passport clamped between her teeth as she marched into my apartment with the cat basket. It wasn't the time to wonder how she'd evaded the security system on the main doors — we've all got a few Deep Dark Secrets in this family, and Nessa's clearly incorporates stealth. 'So, he's staying here for a few days,' she'd finished off, quite triumphantly.

I'd opened my mouth to argue, but I knew my protests were all in vain.

And right now I have to go to do a

talk about pirates and history to a group of kids about a skeleton that was found in their school playground a little while ago. I'm dressed thematically, but I don't think Schubert is an appropriate accessory.

'William, William, William,' says my brother, patting me patronisingly on the arm. 'Us elder McCreadies are too wise to fall for our wee sister's wiles. You, Billy, are the middle child and thus must suffer.' Then he snorts with laughter again. *I think I hate him.* 'Do you know, Mazza,' he continues, turning to Maria, 'Isla once had her car keys eaten by a dog called Bono? And her house keys were *on the same fob*!'

'Wow,' says Maria, nodding sagely. 'Bono has a *lot* to answer for.'

Isla is Hugo's partner and owns a pet portrait and grooming business. She loves Schubert.

I can almost feel the light bulb going *pop* above my head. 'How would Isla like to look after Schubert this afternoon? She loves Schubert.'

'She's also pregnant and can't lift heavy things,' responds Hugo so quickly that it sounds like he'd already planned that answer, just in case the situation arose. 'Schubert is heavy.'

'Mow wow.'

We ignore the indignant grumble and glare at one another.

'She's only a little bit pregnant. Like half an hour pregnant. She can deal with Schubert. She's at work, isn't she?'

'She is three and a half months pregnant. She is not taking on Schubert for you.'

I sense the conversation is at an end, but I decide to try and state my case again anyway. 'Look. I have to go and talk to kids about pirates, and pirates don't have cats — '

'They do. They have feral cats on board the ships. Pretty sure they go ratting and stuff.'

I turn as a female voice I don't recognise enters our conversation. She has a West Country accent.

'And yeah. Black cats. They would

have been awesomely cool if you were a pirate. Good luck. Cats are good.' The woman nods, as if that's the end of the matter. But clearly it's not. 'Cool outfit,' she says. 'Rocking that Bono look.' I stare at her and see a smirk twitching around her lips. She's clearly been party to this whole ridiculous conversation.

'Mow wow,' says Schubert approvingly. The woman has long, dark hair with bright red streaks running through it. I can't tell if they're hair extensions or just streaks of dye.

She's wearing a grungy old green coat that looks like army surplus, a black choker and a T-shirt with a skull on it, over black leggings. She's got a laptop bag slung over her shoulder, biker boots on, and a ring through her bottom lip.

'I am *not* Bono.' *How many times do I have to tell people this?*

'Whatever.' She shrugs and grins and moves towards the counter, where she orders a black coffee and a slice of apple tart with cream. But she's not finished yet. She studies me for a moment with

10

eyes the colour of the blackest espresso. Her eyelids are shaded with smoky blues and greys and outlined in thick black eyeliner. She's stunning, actually. 'Just Jack Sparrow had facial hair and you . . . don't.' She indicates a circle with her finger around her face as if to prove a point. 'Bono. Clean shaven. Mostly. Thanks.' She takes the cup and plate from Maria.

I'm speechless.

Then I turn to Hugo and plead once more. 'Schubert. Take him. Please.'

'No.' His answer is final, and I do feel as if I'm stuffed. I look at the Beast. At least he's got a bandana on. Maybe I can pass him off as a ship's cat? He doesn't really look as if he would be lithe enough to chase a bloody rat, though.

'Uncle Hugo! Uncle Billy!' There's a yell from behind me, and I turn to see my niece Isabel bursting through the door of Thistledean Café. 'Hey Mazza. Isla said you were short-staffed so Uncle Hugo was helping out today. You want me to do anything at the weekend? For

11

pocket money and shit?'

'Don't swear,' we all say automatically. Isa is our brother Scott's eldest daughter. She's a teenager. Say no more. It also explains why Hugo is here, if he's been drafted in at short notice.

But I jump on the request. 'Yes. But not this weekend. Can you look after Schubert this afternoon? Please?'

Isa stares at me strangely. 'I'm at school. This is my officially allocated travelling time. I have to be somewhere, and I chose to travel there via this café. So no.' She seems to do a double take and points at me. 'You look like an ageing rock star.'

'I'm a pirate! Please. Someone believe me when I say I'm a sodding pirate.'

'Don't swear, Uncle Billy,' she says in a prim little voice and hitches her school bag over her shoulder. 'Why are you dressed like *that*, anyway?'

'I have to go to a school and talk about pirates.'

'Oh! Is it the Newhaven pirate? He is soooo cool.'

'Aye. That's the one.'

'Maggie is going to be there.'

Maggie May is her little sister. Maggie May is three. I presume she's going on a nursery trip. I didn't realise nursery kids were involved, and I feel my shoulders literally sag. *Maggie. And Schubert. What could be better?*

Lexie

I stir my coffee thoughtfully and listen to the discussion going on between the people at the counter. The more I look at the pirate, the more I think he actually does look rather dashing.

A bit wild and a bit cool.

I like it.

He's maybe not truly piratical, but he's not bad in that outfit. I decide that I'd quite like another coffee. So, I swig back the cuppa I've got, quite quickly, and get up even more quickly as my head goes a bit *woo woo woo* from the caffeine and the sudden movement. Then I go back to the counter.

I'm not doing this because the pirate is still there. Not at all.

Actually, the pirate smells pretty good too. I like his aftershave. It's kind of earthy and citrusy, which isn't a bad combination. He probably smells a shed load better than a real pirate would.

He's still arguing with the teenager with the cool red hair, though, and the cat is still looking kind of superior.

'No, Isabel. I can't do this *even more* if Mags is there!'

The girl makes a sound like *pshaw* and flicks her red hair back over her shoulder. 'It's not like they're letting the little ones go without supervision, Uncle Billy. Some of the Buddies are going too.'

'Oh God. Isa. Are you a Buddy? For Mags' nursery?'

The teenager grins. 'Aye. Surprise!' She makes jazz hands and dances a little jig. 'That's where I'm travelling to, on my allocated travelling time. To Mags' nursery. I'm a-comin' to see ya! And don't forget you've got us for tea tonight as well!'

'Oh Godddddddd!'

'Mow wow.' The cat, at least, seems pleased.

'Your cat seems happy about it.' I grin up at the pirate. 'Sorry. I've got an abiding interest in pirates. Especially the Newhaven guy. I was kind of excited to hear they'd found a real live pirate's skeleton. I'm not eavesdropping. I'm really not. But — is it, like, a *private* thing? Like a talk just for kids?'

The actual living and breathing pirate stares down at me in confusion and looks a bit thrown. 'Ummm . . . no. No. It's a public talk. But it's in the playground of a school, where they found him. So the bairns get in for free, and the others have to pay a fiver.'

'A fiver is good.' I nod. 'What time is that?'

'It's sold out. Ticket only.' There's a pause as our eyes meet, and it feels a little weird and a little intimate but not unpleasant. Certainly not unpleasant. 'Sorry.'

'Oh. Okay.'

'Mow wow.'

The pirate's attention is drawn back to the cat, who shuffles his bulk around and sits down at a different angle with a hearty *flumph*.

Then there's the sound of a mobile phone ringing and everybody does that thing where, once they've realised it's not their phone, they look around to see whose it is.

'Bugger.' The pirate looks down at a leather satchel thing on the counter. 'Sorry.' He rummages and pulls out a phone. 'Hello, Nessa. To what do I owe this pleasure?'

2

Billy

Nessa chooses her moments. Always. Perfectly in sync with whatever I'm doing that does *not* concern her whatsoever.

'William!' Her voice drips honey, which immediately alerts me to the fact she's not being genuine at all. 'My favourite brother. How *are* you?'

'I am not your favourite brother. You've got a twin. He should be your favourite. He is most like you, so he's the best person to look after Schubert — '

She cuts me off like the leafy bit on a carrot. 'Alfie is busy. And you are my favourite brother. My favourite . . . *piratical* brother!' Her voice is falsely bright and I roll my eyes.

'What do you want, Nessa? What do you *want*?'

'I forgot to tell Hugo something. Is he there?'

I stare at the phone in my hand. Then

17

I look back at Hugo in confusion, and he's making pointy little gestures with his fingers, silently going *Ha ha you got the phone call! And the cat! You've still got the bloody cat!*

I roll my eyes again and look back at the phone. 'Nessa, you could have rung him directly. You didn't need to ring me.'

'Oh, but I did. How's Schubert?'

'Schubert is fine.' I glare at the Beast at my feet who's found something disgusting to lick off the floor. I think it might be coffee grounds, so I try to move him away with my foot because it can't be good for him, but it's like pushing your toes into blancmange and he only bends slightly in the middle like a banana. His tongue does not cease in its quest. His purring is definitely getting a bit louder and a bit more wired, though.

'Good, good. I knew he would not be an encumbrance to you, in your Important Role today.' I wrinkle my nose in disgust. Nessa has this annoying habit of sounding pious and speaking in Capital Letters when she wants to make a point.

'He is a bloody big encumbrance, thank you. I have nobody to look after him when I do the talk, and I can't take him with me. He'll need attention, and I need to concentrate on the talk.' I try a different tactic. 'He'll be neglected.'

'No, he won't.'

'Yes, he will.'

'No. He *won't*.'

'Nessa!'

'Billy. Now — Billy, look to your right, please.'

I blink and turn to my right. The girl with the grungy coat and the pretty sloe-black eyes is standing there, looking curious. As well she might. Her coffee seems to be forgotten; Maria put it on the counter ages ago and the steam is already abating. But she hasn't touched it.

'What do you see?'

I clear my throat. 'Nothing.'

'Billy. What do you see?'

'Nothing.'

'Billy. *Who* do you see?'

'Nobody.' I feel my cheeks heat up as

my eyes meet the girl's again.

'Billy . . . ' The voice is warning. 'I haven't got all day. Jude and Guy are waiting for us.'

Jude and Guy? Does Nessa mean Jude Law and Guy Ritchie?

'Oh. And Tom.' *Tom?* Who is she on about? Tom Hardy? Tom Hiddleston? Who the hell knows, with my sister?

I sigh. 'I don't get where you're coming from, Nessa.'

'Whom,' she enunciates, slowly and clearly, and, yes, piously, 'is standing to your right?'

I give up. 'A customer.'

'Expand.'

'A customer! A girl. For God's sake, Nessa.'

'Does she look nice?'

I clear my throat again. 'Yes. Very much so.'

'Does she like Schubert?'

I look, and the girl has actually bent down now to ruffle the Beast between his ears. Schubert is purring.

'Yes,' I capitulate. 'She does.'

'And does Schubert look as if he likes her?'

'Yes.'

'Excellent. Now, please put Hugo on.'

I shrug and hand the phone to Hugo. He looks horrified, but I thrust the thing at him so he has to take it. By now, Maria has shoved the top of her apron into her mouth and looks as if she's trying not to shriek with laughter, judging by the way her shoulders are shaking and the silent tears that are running down her cheeks.

'Nessa.' My older brother sounds contrite. Defeated, almost. Our little sister has managed to track him down too. And who knows? She may be asking him to take Schubert for me for a couple of hours. Oh, how wonderful that would be . . .

'Yes. Yes. Okay.' Hugo runs his fingers back and forth across the top of the counter, looking shifty. Almost as if he's getting scolded. 'Okay. Yes. I will.' Then he ducks down to the shelf below the cakes and comes up with an envelope in his hand. 'I've got it.' He looks at it, then looks at me, then shrugs. 'Yes. It says *Billy*. Yes. I will.' He hands it across to me and then gives the phone back too.

I stare at him and take the letter. Then I realise I have no spare hands to let go of Schubert's lead. I clumsily hand the lead over to Hugo, and Schubert is dragged, ever so slightly, closer towards the counter. His feet scrabble behind him, most indignantly, as he moves across the slippery floor and comes to rest beside the glass frontage. I bet he looks weird from the other side, with his fur all squashed. He's still stretching though, his tongue attempting to hoover up the coffee grounds in a most disgusting fashion.

I take the phone back. 'Hello, Nessa.'

'Hello, Billy. Now, would you please open the envelope? Thank you.'

'What the —' But I haven't known Nessa all my life without realising it's pointless to argue with her. So, I balance the phone in the crook of my neck and open it.

I stare at the small, rectangular piece of card in my hand. It's a ticket. A ticket for the talk I'm doing this afternoon about the Newhaven pirate. The talk that's sold out.

'It's a ticket for the talk.' I'm confused and stare at it.

'Yes. That's right. Now. If the lady on your right looks nice, and Schubert likes her and she likes Schubert, I need you to offer her the ticket and ask her if she wants to go to the talk, on the proviso that she looks after my wee cat for the duration of it.'

There's a silence. A silence almost as weighty as Nessa's 'wee cat'.

'Go on,' my sister urges. 'Ask her.'

I clear my throat again. 'Ummm . . . excuse me?'

The girl looks up at me, still curiously. 'You're excused.' She stands up, wipes her hand down her coat, and I see several black Schubert hairs float to the floor.

'Thanks. But ummm . . . we seem to have a spare ticket for the talk after all.' I flap it uselessly in front of her. 'My sister, ummmm, couldn't make it. So, she suggested I offer it to . . . to . . . someone who liked cats and ummmm . . . liked pirates.' *God, I sound gormless.* 'She said she was happy for . . . that some-one . . . to attend the talk instead of her. As long as they . . . ummmm . . . looked after . . . ummm . . . the cat. Her cat.' I jiggle the lead and Schubert growls in mild protest. 'This cat. Schubert.'

She stares at me and, for a moment, I think she'd be well within her rights to slap me. All she wanted was a coffee, and now I'm asking her to look after a cat she's never met, for a woman she's never met — and to be told to look after a cat she's never met, for a woman she's never met, by a man she's never met, is just 'cray-cray' as Isabel would say.

There's a pause and I start to formu-late a wiggling-out-of-it sentence, then she grins. 'Okay. Cool. I'd love to. I'm Lexie, by the way. Lexie Farrington.'

She holds her hand out, and I drop the ticket on the counter and shake it. 'Oh. Cool. Yes. I'm Billy. Billy McCreadie.'

'Cool.' She grins at me. 'What time does it start?'

'Can you be there at one? The talk starts at half past.'

'I can indeed. Perfect timing. I've got some stuff to do first, so I'll see you there.'

'Do you promise?' Because if she doesn't promise, I will probably have to look after Schubert myself and I won't be happy. Isa will have to take him, regardless of her Buddying duties. Promises mean a lot to me. I don't break them.

'I promise.' She holds her hand out again and shakes mine solemnly. 'I'd spit on my hand first, but that's probably socially unacceptable when we've only just met.'

I laugh, and I do believe she'll be there. I really do. 'Just a bit. Your word is good enough for now. Here's the ticket.'

'I'll see you there.' She leans down and rumples Schubert's fur a bit more. 'See *you* soon, my lovely.' As she walks off with her half-cold coffee, the smile is still on my lips.

'She must really love U2,' mutters Hugo, who has seemingly recovered from his conversation with Nessa.

Which reminds me, Nessa is still on the end of my phone. 'Nessa? It's okay. She's looking after him.'

'And her name?' asks Nessa. 'I need to know her name.'

'Lexie. Lexie Farrington.' I enjoy the way the words sound coming out of my mouth.

'Lexie. Splendid. Okay. I love you, Billy. Put me on to Hugo again, please.'

I silently hand the phone over and Hugo's face pales, then he relaxes a bit. 'Love you too, Nessa,' he says. Then he pauses, nods and comes around the front of the counter. He's still got Schubert on the lead so it takes a bit of manoeuvring, but I'm not going to offer to help him. Then he holds the phone down to Schubert's fur, around about where his ear would be.

'Mow wow,' says Schubert after a moment, then he purrs. Then he licks my phone and I pull a face.

God. Now the screen will smell of tuna. And coffee.

Because as Hugo silently hands the phone back to me, I see there are a few rancid coffee grounds in the streak of saliva. *Yep. Definitely coffee.*

Good grief.

Lexie

I'm waiting, as promised, by the gates of the school that Billy McCreadie is going to do his talk at. It looks like a nice school. Very old, and all made of lovely stonework. It's close to the harbour and as I wait, I sniff the air and the unmistakeable tang of salt comes tickling through my nose. There are cobbles on the road and the sound of gulls in my ears, and I decide I like it here. I like it very much.

I must admit, I quite like the sea air anyway — there are some beautiful coastlines I've travelled to. It's nice to stay by the sea for a little while, but then I'm off to the next job, the next adventure. I might head inland for a bit next; see what the moors and the Dales are like as I pass through them. I might stay for a bit, I might not. It all depends if the place calls to me, and nowhere has really *called* to me for a while. Which is why it's nice to feel more at home here in Edinburgh. I could definitely stay here for a bit.

There are already some people heading into the school yard, and someone has put piratical bunting up on the fence, each little bunting triangle depicting something like a skull and cross bones, or a sailing ship or a treasure chest There's a banner advertising the event as well. *William McCreadie is*, it says, *a local tour guide with an interest in the history of the area*, then it names the company he works for. I grin. They do haunted graveyard tours as well, which I decide is very much on my agenda for my sojourn in Edinburgh. Billy most certainly looks the part of a pirate — okay, with maybe a smattering of *Joshua Tree* Bono sprinkled in there. I find myself wondering if he'll do the same sort of thing for the haunted graveyard tours.

Maybe he'll dress as a highwayman or a vampire? Either of those would be pretty cool, but I don't know whether there are any famous iterations of highwaymen or vampires in Scotland. I screw my nose up as I think about it.

A moment later, I realise I must look pretty odd with a screwed-up nose because Billy's suddenly there, right next to me, half-smiling. 'Am I disturbing anything? You look deep in thought.'

'Oh! Yes. That's my thinking face. Sorry. I was thinking about highwaymen and vampires . . . and if there are any famous Scottish ones.' I feel my cheeks flush. He doesn't need to know I'm imagining him in the outfits.

'Scottish highwaymen. Well.' He pulls a face to match mine and holds up his hand — the hand that is not holding a purple lead with a cat on the end of it — and counts them off: 'I've a few you can be going on with. Gilderoy, born Patrick McGregor, died 1636, given the dubious honour of being hung on a gibbet higher than his friends. It's quite possible his body was displayed around here.' He nods in the direction of the harbour, and the single hooped earring in his left ear wobbles a bit. 'In one version of his life, his body was taken, they say, still in chains, to be exhibited on another gibbet between Edinburgh and Leith to warn other bad boys. Then there's Sawney Douglas — pal of the very wonderful Claude Duval, acted like an idiot in prison, died 1664 carrying a copy of the ballad 'Chevy Chase' and not a prayer book. Your basic thug, I think. And James MacLaine. Possibly born Scottish, lived in Dublin, died at Tyburn in 1750 at about twenty-six years old — poor guy was made an example of, but it didn't stop the ladies visiting him in prison and pleading for his release.' He grins, suddenly. 'I like MacLaine. Didn't get it quite right, though.'

'I think I'd like him too.' I laugh. 'And vampires?'

'There *are* a few stories. Glamis Castle has a vampire legend. You've got our very beautiful banshees who have many of the same characteristics. And even here, in Edinburgh, there are a couple of stories. A medical student died mysteriously of puncture wounds in a supposedly haunted hotel in about 1915, and a few years earlier, around about 1899 in Princes Street, there was something weird that attacked a horse.'

'Oh no!' I shiver, imagining it all. 'The poor student! The poor *horse*!'

'It's okay. The horse survived.'

'The poor young guy in the hotel didn't, though!'

'True.' He looks contrite for a moment before speaking again. 'So, does that answer your questions? I've got a bit of useless knowledge stored up here.' He taps the side of his head.

'I suspect you'll need it, for your job.'

I point to the banner, where it says what he does, and he nods. 'Aye. It's a good job. One of my best.'

He indicates that we should head into the yard and I fall into step with him, the cat prancing, as well as he can prance, in front of us. It's more like the swaying a

31

really obese belly dancer might do, to be honest.

We come to a standstill and Billy looks at the lead in his hand, then looks at me, almost apologetically. 'I guess this where I have to leave you with Schubert. I'm really, really sorry. But, if it's any consolation, at least you'll get into the talk. Like I said, we were all sold out.'

'I'm sure we'll be fine.' I take the lead from him and sit down on a chair that's clearly borrowed from the primary school as my knees are up under my chin, and my bum is level with Schubert's head. The chairs are arranged in a sort of horseshoe shape, in rows facing the entrance door. They're set far enough back so that the children can sit down cross-legged in front of us on loads of lovely, bright-coloured woolly rugs.

I'm quite close to the front of the horseshoe, and the nursery kids and their Buddies have all slunk in now. I can see redheaded Isabel and another little red-haired girl who looks just like her sitting together. Isabel looks at me and waves, then points at Schubert and gives me a thumbs up.

Schubert looks at her, inclines his head regally, then studies me curiously before climbing up onto my lap. I catch my breath and groan inwardly as he snuggles into me; he's not a light-weight animal. Then he closes his eyes and begins to snore gently.

And I couldn't move away, even if I wanted to — but I don't want to, as by now Billy McCreadie, Pirate/Bono extraordinaire, has begun to talk, and already he has the audience rapt.

Billy

I think that went quite well, to be honest. You never know what sort of reception you'll get. Once I did a tour, and when I turned around half the group had buggered off into a pub. It was the oldest pub in Edinburgh, but still. It was downright rude.

I have some dubious, shall we say,

'friends', who might have made their evening unforgettable in that old pub. I have no control over what they do; we speak very infrequently, and they tend to keep to the shadows. But they're good people to know and enjoy a bit of fun. I must ask them what happened next time I'm in there for a pint. Discreetly, though.

'Not bad, Uncle Billy. Not bad at all.' Back in the school yard, Isa has sloped up next to me and is standing with her hands on her hips.

Mini-me-Mags is standing in the same position. 'Not bad,' she parrots. 'Good.' Then she flings her arms out to the side exuberantly. *'Pirates*!' She grins at me, and it's a grin you can't resist. She's already got that 'Winning McCreadie Smile' going on, clearly inherited from Scott.

'Yes. Pirates, Mags.' I grin and lean down, chucking her under the chin. 'Now, I'm sure you have to go with your Buddy here back to nursery. I'll see you soon, okay?'

'Uncle Billy,' she says, her hands behind her back now. 'Who 'Bono'?'

She frowns and Isabel snorts with laughter. 'Nice one,' she says and pats her sister's head.

'You've taught her well,' I say, frowning back at them. 'Now shoo. Away ye gan! Avast ye, landlubbers!' I put on a broad Scottish, hopefully piratical, accent and indicate that they should leave by batting my hands in their direction.

'Not *entirely* sure that's the correct terminology,' says Isa with a superior sniff. Then she grins. 'Think 'avast ye' means to hold on, but then what do I know?'

'Then just go. Nail your colours to the mast and go.'

'Again. Not *entirely* sure — '

I glare at her.

'Okay! Okay. I'm going. Off to join the crocodile.' Isa rolls her eyes and grabs Mags by the hand, then joins a swarm of pre-schoolers in a wobbly crocodile shape. They waddle off, Isa waving over her shoulder and giving me thumbs up gestures in Lexie Farrington's direction.

I shake my head and walk over to Lexie. She's looking a wee bit flattened, and I notice Schubert is drooling onto her lap as he squashes her into a seat made for hobbits.

'Let me rescue you.' I relieve her of Schubert's lead. He wakes up and moans, then shuffles off her lap and slithers to the floor.

'Thank you!' She stands up, a little stiffly, and her green coat is covered in more black hairs. She dusts herself down and jumps from foot to foot, obviously trying to get some life back into the limbs that Schubert cut the blood supply off to. The buckles and zips on her biker boots rattle a bit. 'That was so interesting. Thank you.' She smiles at me. 'What a find.'

'I know.' The skeleton was, as I had explained in the talk, found when they were doing some extension works to the school, and they dated him back to the sixteenth century.

Due to the location, the experts think he's a pirate that was hung in the docks and left on display — again, to deter other piratical types. Regardless of the truth, it's a swashbuckling tale and the audience today have loved it.

'Look,' I say. 'Let me thank *you* for looking after Schubert. How about a coffee?'

'Oh, he was no bother!' She studies me, then smiles. 'But I'm not going to turn a coffee down. Is there anywhere around here we can go?'

'Yes. Just down there.' I gesture along the street. 'Just let me say my farewells to the guys here and I'll be there in a second.' I delve into my pockets — because yes, I have hidden pockets in my outfit; handy for mobile phones, keys, wallets and flyers about the latest haunted graveyard tour. I know the kids here are too young, but the parents might like it — or the guests that are, even now, still milling around and looking at the CGI image of the pirate's recreated face, which is still propped up behind where I was talking. 'I've got some shameless advertising to do. There's a tour tomorrow night, and

I'm drumming some trade up.'

'Okay.' Lexie smiles and shrugs her shoulders. 'I'll just wait here. Shall I . . . ?' She gestures to Schubert's lead and I hand it back to her.

'Great.' I smile back and hand-deliver those leaflets just as fast as I can. I really don't want to take the chance that she'll run off.

Although, anchored by Schubert and his purple lead, that scenario is unlikely.

3

Lexie

We're sitting in, of all places, a fish and chip restaurant. We've got pots of tea in front of us and a bowl of chips each. They're covered with salt and vinegar, and very delicious. Schubert has some fish bites which he seems extremely happy about, I have to say.

I pour out my third cup of tea and reflect on how easy Billy has been to talk to. He's an absolute mine of information about the area, and I'm absorbing it all like a sea-sponge. I guess I've got a vested interest in the piratical history of this place as it's part of my current research.

'So, have you had a few jobs, then?' I ask him as I stir sugar into my tea. 'Because you're really good at this one.'

'One or two.' He smiles, and it's a very cheeky smile. 'I've done quite a bit of stuff, including working in a seaside town

39

café for a summer season. Somewhere a bit like this in fact, but on the north east coast of England. I rented a caravan on a site overlooking a lighthouse, and it was a pretty cool place to be. I then ended up in the fairground on the ghost train, of all things. That was fun. Oh, and I was briefly a mechanic at a steam museum down in Norfolk. Then I took that skill to a garage, back up here, and ended up being a car salesman for a bit. I've done other things too in between. I've tried a *lot* of jobs.'

'And the worst one was?'

'The car salesman.'

'And the best?'

'This one. So far. Unless I get bored with it. Well — having said that, I'm already thinking about the next one. I'm thinking about becoming a history teacher. That sounds good, doesn't it?' He looks sidelong at me. 'I'd get to teach kids and talk about history all day. I can do the history tours alongside it for a bit, because I'll need to do a teaching qualification first.'

'Sounds good. I've had a few jobs too. Currently I'm an archivist, and I do a little bit of genealogy in the side. My worst job was in an office doing accounts. So boring. I was a waitress in an artisan bakery in Primrose Hill, in London, for a bit. That was good. I learned a lot about cakes. I can make a pretty good cake; make it a generous catering size, and edible as well. There's a certain art to that, I reckon. Oh, I did a stint in a costume museum too, nearer home. Textiles. Costume collections. Loved, loved, *loved* that one. My degree is in fashion, so yeah, that was cool. I've kind of picked up other work along the way. I rock up somewhere, take a job and see how it goes. Not one for putting down roots, really. I tell myself there's too much of the world to see, but it's not always enough. Okay . . . I'm weird.' I realise I'm rambling.

'Not weird. Interesting, I'd say. But definitely not weird. What do you do now?'

'I'm erring towards genealogy. It's a

41

bit of a sideline, because, as I say, I currently work in an archive collection. One day I'll get back into the fashion side of things, but I moved away from home again, and they didn't have a fashion museum for me to work in where I went.' I scowl. Sometimes, I hate my nomadic habits. I can't seem to settle anywhere, and I'm always trying new stuff. New towns, new jobs, new people. I start to feel like I'm missing out on something else. And then I wonder why I can't keep a relationship going. I must have some travelling genes in me somewhere.

'Your jobs all sound amazing.' Billy's voice brings me back to Newhaven. 'Lots of variety.'

'It's the spice of life.' I grin. 'Yours sound good too. Maybe not the car salesman.'

'Yeah. It was a bit too much like cheating people out of their hard-earned cash. Not my thing. Your accounts one sounds bad too.'

'Beyond bad.' I frown. *I really hated that job.*

'So, what's your genealogy bringing you up here for? Is it for you or for someone else?'

'For me, mainly. I think my family has links up here. That's what I need to discover.'

'Awesome. Well, if you're around tomorrow evening, we've got a tour on at Greyfriars Kirkyard — you know, the old cemetery? We're not the only company who does the tours, but, dare I say it, I'm the best guide out of the lot of them.'

He winks and I burst out laughing. As well as feel slightly stunned by the teasing light in his green eyes, the general piratical look is enhanced. He really is very sexy in that garb.

'Yeah. I think I'm free tomorrow. I booked two-and a-bit weeks off work, and this is just the start of it. A graveyard tour sounds cool and you know, I *had* thought about doing one anyway. I do like a cemetery or two. Not in a weird way, you understand,' I add hurriedly. 'I found a good one at a corner of

Princes Street earlier. Lots of good stuff in there . . . ' I let the words trail off. It *did* sound weird, really.

'That's fine. I like them too. Okay — well, I really hate to have to do this, but I need to get back.' He scowls a little. 'I have my nieces coming for tea — those two little monsters you saw before — so I should go and sort that out. And at least he — ' he gestures to Schubert who is licking his paws delicately after his meal ' — will be there to amuse them until my sister comes back tonight. And as soon as that plane lands and she sets foot in her house, the Beast is going home. Mags, that's the little one, keeps trying to dress him up. There are a limited number of people who can do that to Schubert, and she's one of them. Nessa put that bandana on him days ago, but I'll have to get Isabel or Mags to take it off. Probably Mags.'

'Well done, Mags!' I lean down and rub Schubert's furry head again and he flicks his ear listlessly, then mutters 'mow wow' in acknowledgement.

He is quite a funky cat, actually. Lots of personality.

I like that in a cat. I really do.

Billy

'So, Uncle Billy,' says Isabel, sprawled all over my sofa with her phone in her hand and her fingers flying over the screen, 'on a scale of zero to O-M-G, how fanciable do you reckon that girl was who looked after Schubert?'

Her eyes don't even leave the display. Rather, when she realises she isn't getting a response, they swivel around like something out of a horror movie and I watch, fascinated.

'Isabel McCreadie. That's inappropriate.'

''s not.'

''tis.'

She rolls those eyes and flops around so she's facing me properly. 'She's really pretty. And she was *into* you.'

'That's even *worse*! And even more

inappropriate.'

'I dunno. She might like Bono. Like, secretly, really, *really* like Bono.' She grins and thrusts the phone in my face. And there he is, looking at me, a picture of that good gentleman circa 1987. I look away, as yes, I can see how they think I looked like him in that one video where he's strutting around LA dressed in black leather.

'Don't be stupid.' I try for a withering tone but, at the end of the day, she's a teenage girl and I'm an adult, so I refuse to be drawn into it with her.

'I know you're planning to see her tomorrow night,' says Isa, far too innocently.

'How?' I dart a glance at her.

'Mow wow.' Schubert mutters something from the armchair.

'Doesn't matter how I know. Just that I do know.' Isabel smirks into her phone screen again and Schubert flumps over. If I didn't know better, it almost sounds like he's singing to himself. He also sounds far too innocent.

I'm not going to go there.

'I think,' announces Isa, 'that *I* shall also be going on that tour.'

'You will not be!'

'Will.'

'Will not.'

'Will.'

I have realised, once again, that I am the adult here and need to shut up.

'Where you going?' Maggie toddles in with a mermaid doll in her hands and climbs onto the armchair next to Schubert. He obligingly shuffles over and then rests his head in her lap. She un-pops a press stud and takes the fake, slip-on tail off the doll, before trying to feed Schubert's furry tail into the little shimmery piece of cloth. The doll's legs look weirdly naked, compared to its fancy sparkly bra thing.

'Out with Uncle Billy. On a tour. Like a talk. Like the talk he did today. But a grown-up talk.'

'You're not coming, Isabel. It's late at night and you need to be in bed.'

'It's seven o'clock, Uncle Billy,' she

47

says witheringly. She definitely sounds more withering than I managed to sound; I have to give her credit for that one. 'I am not in bed at seven. *She* is in bed at seven.' Isabel points her phone at her small sister. 'I just need to tell Mum and Dad I'm going out to Sophie's or something. Joke!' she says, glancing up at me. She has the grace to blush. Last time she lied about where she was, it didn't end well as she got trapped in a burning building until my brother swooped in and pulled her out.

'It's not appropriate,' I say, but then I think, *actually, when did I become a really boring adult?* I can't put my finger on it.

And why isn't it appropriate? It's just a history talk with a bit of added spookiness.

And do you know what? Thinking about it, I don't want to be a really boring adult.

'Okay.' I sigh and look at her. 'The minimum age is fourteen.'

'Me.' She puts her hand up in the air but doesn't look away from the phone screen as the mobile is clearly sucking her in again.

'You. Right. If your mum and dad agree, you can come. But you need to behave. I can't be looking after you and doing a tour. You have to be sensible.'

'Can I bring a flask of tea for the break? Tea is very sensible. *Uber* sensible. Tea is *good*. And it might get a bit chilly.'

'You can bring a flask of tea. *If* you can come.'

'Oh, I'll be able to.' She nods confidently, and she reminds me of a red-haired version of Nessa.

'We will see.' I fold my arms and study her.

Mags shoves her face into Schubert's fur and makes kissy noises. 'She will,' the little one says in a muffled voice. 'She very will.'

* * *

She very can. I'm not impressed with my brother or his wife; they said they'd 'consider it', and I wrongly assumed by 'considering it' they basically meant 'no'. In my day, when my parents said 'we'll see', it was never going to turn out the way we wanted it. I'm not convinced having Isa at the talk is a good idea, but I really was hoping I wouldn't be the one who had to tell her that.

Oh well.

We'll see.

Today is Saturday, and we've all somehow convened at Nessa's house. She rang me to say she'd acquired a new history book and asked whether I'd like to come and collect it. She could have given it to me last night when I brought her bloody cat home. And then at some point, she also rang Scott and offered to babysit the girls for the day if he and Liza wanted to go to a pop-up vintage fayre that had started up in the Assembly Rooms.

Liza is a demon for upcycling and Scott is an interior designer, so they jumped at the chance to have a look at the fayre. They both made something up about wanting to see the latest styles, but my argument was if it's fifties and sixties stuff, how can it be the latest style?

'This from the 1987 Bono-lookalike,' said Scott, but I chose to ignore that comment.

To give them their due, they did say babysitting wasn't required, and they'd be fine with the girls there. However, Isa whinged and moaned and stomped around a bit, saying she'd rather see Schubert and play in Nessa's basement — and, of course, Maggie copied her older sister and did some miniature stomping — so it ended up being easiest all round if Nessa took them.

Now, I'm sitting on the sofa nursing a cup of tea and being side-eyed by the Beast, as I presume I've got his seat.

'You have Schubert's seat,' says Nessa and stares at me until I shuffle across and squeeze myself as far up against the armrest as I can get.

Scott is oblivious, as he only has eyes for Liza. She's had some sort of makeover at the fayre, and is currently wearing a 1960s Twiggy-style mini dress and has her hair done in a kind of Brigitte

Bardot beehive thing. Liza's a redhead, like Isabel and Maggie, so she's more Jean Shrimpton than Bardot, but still, she looks good. Scott is practically dribbling. So, the seating issue has passed him over. I'm a little annoyed as I thought I could rely on someone to take my side.

Ewan, Nessa's partner, only has eyes for my wild-haired sister, and I'm feeling a bit of a fifth wheel. I pick up the book Nessa's given me, just so I don't have to look at these loved up couples around me. A vision of Lexie Farrington flits into my mind and out again. Yeah, she's lovely. She is. But she's not *here*, is she?

'That book is all about pirates,' says Nessa, interrupting my grumpy mood and *flumph*-ing down next to me. Schubert does a kind of Mexican wave, his fur and fat rippling as he bounces up and down on the sofa, settling at length back into a messy black heap.

'Pirates?' I look at her and raise my eyebrows. 'Not Bono? Not a biography of U2 or anything like that?'

'Why would I do that?' She looks at

me, disgusted. I hope she's going to say something about me not looking like Bono. 'U2 are *Irish*, not Scottish. But I did think for your next birthday I could — '

'No Nessa. Just stop with the Bono stuff. Please.' I wave the book. 'This. This is the look I was going for. See? Famous pirates. Famous *Scottish* pirates.'

'Well, of course, William.' She pats my hand. 'See? Captain Kidd is in there — Captain *William* Kidd.' She smiles at me beatifically. 'And Sir Andrew Barton.'

'Captain Kidd.' I nod. I do feel an affinity for that particular pirate. We share a name for a start.

'Mow wow?' Schubert looks up at Nessa questioningly.

'No, darling,' she says, addressing the Beast. 'He doesn't mean Billy the Kid. He's a cowboy. This is Captain *William* Kidd. A piratical gentleman.'

I shake my head. *I'm not even going there.* Nessa is probably winding me up and Schubert said nothing of the sort.

'Mow wow.'

He seems to mutter something again and Nessa sniggers. 'No. Not Bono.'

I really am not going to show her I've heard. Because I do think she's winding me up now, I really do.

To make sure she absolutely knows I'm not listening, or taking any notice whatsoever of what Schubert allegedly has or has not said, I flick through the book. It does actually look quite good.

'I still feel sorry for Captain Kidd.' I point to the well-copied engraving of the poor bloke hanging in his gibbet. 'It's unfortunate that he started sailing as a privateer, just when pirates and privateers became outlaws.'

'Really?' Nessa leans over to get a better look at the gory picture.

'Really.' I shove the book towards her as her hair is up my nose. 'I believe he was travelling around India as a pirate, forced into it by his crew, when they changed the laws. He didn't know.'

'That is *very* unfortunate.' Nessa stares at the picture then grimaces. 'It says here he was hanged twice.'

'Aye. The first rope broke.' I shudder. 'Imagine that. Thinking you've got off, and then they string you up again.'

'Ugh!' Nessa slams the book shut. 'Horrid. What about his crew? The ones that weren't mean mutineers?'

'I don't know.' I grin at her. 'I haven't read the book yet.'

'What about *girl* pirates?' Isabel bursts through the door, obviously after ear-wigging on the conversation for a while. 'There were *girl* pirates, too. Like Anne Bonny. And Mary Read.'

'*Girl* pirates,' echoes Maggie, tumbling in after Isa. 'Arrr. Arrr.' Maggie has obviously decided to talk like a pirate. She clambers on the sofa, and, of course, bloody Schubert moves for *her*, then lays his head lovingly in her lap yet a-bloody-gain. 'Ahhh Schubert. Scamp *loves* you. And *I* love you. We *all* love you.' Scamp is Isa and Maggie's pet cat. I doubt Scamp loves Schubert to that extent, but hey ho.

Regardless, I'm pretty glad I closed the book on poor old Cap'n Kidd dangling in his gibbet. I remember it gave my younger brother, Alfie, nightmares for ages when he was a child.

Maybe I shouldn't have cut it out and used it as a bookmark in his prized copy of *The Incredible Adventures of Professor Branestawm*.

'Urgh, Mum, what on *earth* are you dressed in?' Isa suddenly seems to catch sight of Liza.

'It's vintage,' says Liza. 'There's nothing wrong with it. It's in keeping.'

'But you're, like, *old*.' Isabel stares at Liza.

'I am not old. I am mid-thirties. That is *not* old.' Liza is clearly unimpressed by her daughter. She pats her hairdo, to make a point, and crosses her legs. She's wearing thigh-length white PVC boots.

'Your mum looks stunning,' says Scott, 'and if you want to go to that thing tonight with Uncle Billy, then there'll be less of the elderly comments.'

'I don't think you should let her go.' I nip in, seizing the moment, *carpe diem*-ing like the best of them. 'She's

56

being cheeky.'

Isabel rolls her eyes. But then I notice Scotty still looking at Liza and practically drooling. 'No,' he says, 'she can go. Mags, you look sleepy. I think we need to go home and *you* need a nice, early night.'

'Don't want one.'

'Yes you do.'

'Don't.'

'Do.'

I'm glad Scott forgets his status as an adult at times as well.

'Maggie May,' interjects Nessa, 'would you like to stay here tonight? And Isabel? You too?'

'Mow wow?'

'No, darling, Mags won't be sleeping in your basket tonight.'

'Sleeping in the *cat* basket?' Liza squawks.

'Yes. Last time they argued over who got to snuggle Catnip.' Nessa nods sagely, referring to a skanky old soft toy mouse that she swears Schubert can't sleep without. 'So, I think it's best that

Mags has her own bed tonight.' She waves up the stairs vaguely. 'She can have her usual room, it's fine. Isa, you can have yours too, after you come back from your tour with Uncle Billy.'

'Nessa . . . ' Ewan starts to ask something, or comment on something, then obviously decides not to. I cringe inwardly. There's too much stuff going on here tonight. Too many couples wanting to get it on.

Again, Lexie's face floats into my mind and I wonder, briefly, what it would be like to kiss someone with a lip ring.

What it would be like to kiss Lexie Farrington . . .

'Never mind.' Ewan sighs, quietly, but Nessa grins at him.

'It's only one night, Ewan Grainger,' she tells him. Then she leans across to him and I hear her whisper, 'Their rooms are miles away, anyway.'

Ewan visibly brightens, clearly only just remembering that they live in a bloody humongous sodding house. It used to be three flats and they lived one above the other, but they got it converted back into one house when they got together. Nessa turned the basement into her Witchy Consultancy, where she keeps all her herbs and plant products. Isa and Mags love going down there and messing around, making potions and things. Isa's pocket, come to think of it, looks suspiciously bulky, but I pass it off. They're always making perfume and shit.

But I can't take it any more. There's too much sexual tension going on, and I stand up swiftly.

'I'm going home. I need to prepare for tonight. Is Isabel coming then?' I direct my comment to Scott and Liza, willing them to say 'no, don't be daft'.

But they're planning a night of debauchery, I can tell. Liza is already on the Just Eat app, ordering a takeaway and muttering about grabbing a nice bottle of wine on the way home. Scott only has eyes for Liza's legs, so I give up.

'So, I've got your daughter's company at the kirkyard, yes?' I try not to sound bitter.

Scott and Liza both nod absently. 'Yes,' says Scott. 'We're fine with that.'

'I bloody bet you are,' I say. I actually *can't* hide the bitterness in that comment.

'Come along then!' Nessa claps her hands like a school teacher. If I'm ever a school teacher, I won't be bloody doing that sodding thing. 'Isabel, come with me. I have the most perfect outfit for you. Mags, kiss Mummy and Daddy goodnight, and then you can come too. Let's see what story you want tonight . . .'

'Bloody brilliant.' I sit down again.

I give up.

I absolutely do.

Lexie

I'm lurking around the cemetery gates, waiting for Billy to turn up. There's a group of people already here, and one or two of the older ones are staring curiously at me. I suspect my lip-ring

60

is a little out of their comfort zone, and maybe I could have toned down my make-up a bit, but it's Saturday night and I'm out-out, so it's time to bring out the dark, smoky eyes and the heavy black mascara and the cherry-red lipstick. I've tied my hair back, so yes, my tattoo may or may not be visible on the side of my neck, just behind my ear, and my Alice in Chains T-shirt is perhaps not *de rigueur* for people of a certain age. But I am definitely looking forward to this tour.

Like I say, I do like old cemeteries and I've been desperate to visit this one as I've always *wanted* to. If that makes sense? I've read about it, and it's always seemed to resonate with me. Despite my wanderings, it's somewhere I've always felt I needed to explore.

I have to say I'm as excited about this as I was about the pirate talk at the school yesterday.

There's a flurry of excited twittering from a group of ladies dressed sensibly in anoraks, trousers and boots, and perhaps a girlish giggle or two as well. I look towards where they are facing and my jaw practically drops open.

Here comes Billy McCreadie, striding down the road towards us. He's wearing a long, black frock coat, *á la* Mr Darcy, and black leather trousers. Underneath that coat, which is flapping around in a very pleasing manner, is a close-fitting black shirt and a velvety-looking waistcoat. He's got black riding boots on as well. He looks a bit scowly and stormy and — oh my, I like it.

In fact, I can't quite help imagining him emerging out of a swirling mist with a leather waistcoat on, shirtless beneath it, wanging a guitar around his head.

A bit like Bono perhaps?

It would be another good look on Billy, I think.

Like me, his hair is tied back and, it might be my imagination, but underneath the stormy expression it seems like he's looking for someone amongst the crowd. Those green eyes flash with recognition as they meet mine, and a half smile suddenly plays around his lips, softening the very sexy and quite deliciously dangerous aspect of him.

I'd like to think it's me he's looking for, but it's more than likely he's doing a quick head count as he's also carrying a clipboard.

Then I notice that a miniature black-clad figure holding a torch is trailing in his wake. It's only when they get closer that I realise it's his eldest niece, Isabel. She's carrying herself confidently, and it strikes me she's loving the attention. Because, let's face it, all eyes are on Billy, and then, by default, the eyes are sliding curiously to her. There's a huge smile on her face and I can't help but grin back. I reckon she's more than likely the source of Billy's scowly face.

The girl raises her hand and waves at me. 'Good evening,' she cries. 'So pleased you could make it. Now — ' she transfers her attention to the crowd and swipes the clipboard from her uncle ' — may I check your names are all on the list? There should be fifteen of you all together.' Moving around the visitors, she efficiently nods and ticks names off. She comes to me last and her eyes, the same shade of green as his, appraise me. I hold her gaze and appraise her just as much.

'Alexandrina Farrington. You're on the list. Good,' she says, the pen poised. 'But *Alexandrina*?' She looks stunned at my relatively unusual name.

'I prefer Lexie. I don't tend to use the full name. It just that's what's on my PayPal from when I booked.

'Alexandrina — isn't that what Queen Victoria was called? Her nickname was Drina?'

'I believe so.'

'We've done her in history.' A wave of the pen. 'Gladstone and Disraeli. Chartists. Politics and shit — '

'Isabel!' Her uncle is clearly not amused, and he glowers at her. Then he turns to me. 'I'm so sorry. I knew it was a bad idea bringing her.'

I laugh. 'Of course it's not.' I smile at her. 'I prefer people history. Not politics.'

'Damn right,' she mutters and scribbles something on the clipboard. 'Lexie. Cool. That's changed now. Lexie Farrington. Good.' She looks up at Billy. 'You may commence.'

She's dressed as a miniature pirate, I realise — possibly rocking the Anne Bonny look rather than her uncle's Bono look. I'm thinking Billy may be rocking the Adam Ant look tonight, actually — there's definitely an element of dandy highwayman. Whatever it is, it's a bloody good look.

'Thank you.' He turns to the crowd and smiles. There's a kind of collective *ahhhh* as the ladies all smile back at him and all the men mumble 'hello'.

'Let me, first of all, welcome you to Greyfriars Cemetery. Or, Greyfriars Kirkyard as it is better known. The Greyfriars name comes from the Franciscan friary that was once on the site, and the friars of that friary, not surprisingly, wore grey robes. The friary was dissolved in 1560, and the church you can see over there was founded in 1602. It was completed around 1620, which makes it one of the oldest surviving buildings in our beautiful Old Town. It's still used today, and we hold regular services in Gaelic. The cemetery has been in use since the late sixteenth century and was granted a royal sanction to replace the burial ground at St Giles . . . '

I let his voice wash over me, and it's almost hypnotic. He's so very interesting, and soon we're following him around the springy turf and exclaiming at the very beautiful stonework on some of these old tombs and mausoleums. Isabel pulls a face at the mortsafes which look like little cages over some of the graves. I linger to read the inscription on one, and she slides over to me.

'It was to stop Resurrectionists,' she says, pointing at the tombs. 'You know. Because the graverobbers would dig 'em up.' She makes digging motions and pulls another face. We stare at the iron bars quietly. There's a carving on one of the graves; it says *Non omnis moriar*. 'What's that mean?' Isabel jabs at it with her imaginary shovel.

'My Latin is a bit rusty, but I think it says 'Not all of me will die'.' A shiver runs over my shoulders and down my spine when I say those words, and I find I'm staring at it more than is possibly appropriate. 'I wonder what they meant by that?'

'I suppose it depends on who exactly is in there.' Isabel runs her gaze over the iron bars. 'A vampire? They don't like iron, do they?'

'I'm not sure. I think they probably do like it. They drink blood, don't they?'

'Hmm. That's true.'

We stare at the mortsafe a bit longer, and I have to tear myself away from it.

'Anyway. It's time for a cuppa, I think,' says Isa. She turns to me, and I realise she's about the same height as me. I'm not hugely tall, I have to say.

'I'm not sure you're allowed to have breaks in these sorts of things,' I say carefully.

'*Och*, we're allowed. Look.' She nods over to the tour group, and I notice they've split into smaller groups, all with flasks and some with snacks. 'It's about halfway through, you see, so to give my uncle a break and so his voice doesn't go all crackly and croaky, we always have a cuppa break.'

'We, Isabel?' Billy has materialised behind me and if, he hadn't spoken, I would have known he was there regardless because the actual *air* has gone all crackly, never mind his voice. I feel a bit wibbly-wobbly, which is kind of crazy, and I turn around slowly and look up at him. God, he is very close — and I can't stop staring into his eyes. I'm aware there are a few of the older ladies looking across at us curiously.

'We.' Isabel's voice interrupts my staring, and I look back at her as she nods. 'I'm your glamorous assistant today.' She does a theatrical twirl and then raises the flask. There are three plastic cups screwed into one another on the top of it. 'So, let's have a break.'

She unscrews the cups and the lid, and carefully pours out three drinks. She is muttering and grumbling to herself as she does so, and sits down right next to us, cross-legged on the springy grass, as she sets them out in front of her.

'Do we have a choice?' Billy raises his eyebrows and shakes his head. Then he looks at me. 'Can we interest you in some tea?'

'In the absence of my own tea, I'd love some.' I smile up at him, and he grins back.

'Here you go.' Isa thrusts a cup at me and I take it. 'Enjoy it!' She grins and knocks back a glug of her own. 'It's herbal. Less caffeine. More healthy.'

'Cheers.' Billy raises his cup. 'So, how are you finding the tour? I — '

'Oh damn!' Isabel has managed to put her cup down on a tuft of grass, and it's tipped up and emptied all over. The liquid is seeping into the ground and she looks at it, horrified. 'Oh noooooo!'

'Isabel!' Billy says sharply. 'It's only tea. Just get some more. Nobody under . . . there . . . is going to be bothered.'

'But . . . noooo!' She looks at him, terror in her eyes. 'It's . . . it's . . . '

'It's tea, Isabel.'

'It's . . . it's . . .'

'Isabel.' His tone is warning, and I hide a smile. He's doing pretty well, dealing with a teenager.

She gives a dramatic, shuddering sigh. 'Yes. Yes it is. It's just tea.' She rights the cup and carefully pours some more. 'Just tea.'

'Good.' There's a smile lurking around his lips now as he looks at her. 'Because if it wasn't just tea, I think I'd be telling your parents not to allow you to come out with me on my tours any more.'

'Not just tea?' Her voice is small, and she looks at him with huge, worried eyes.

'No.' His brow crinkles a bit. 'Like, if it's alcohol or something. You know?'

'Oh! Oh. Alcohol. Yes.' Isabel nods again, then shakes her head. 'It's not alcohol. Just tea.'

'Okay.' Billy looks at her for a moment again, then shakes his head. 'So, as I was saying, Lexie, are you enjoying the tour?'

'I am! There are some fascinating stories, aren't there?'

'Yes. We can't cover all of them in the

time we've got here tonight. I just have to pick and choose some of the better known ones to satisfy everyone, but, you know, if you're free any other time, just give me a shout and I'll be happy to chat a bit more about it.'

He smiles at me and I find myself nodding. 'Yes. Yes, I'm free.'

'When? When are you free?'

'Ummm . . . I don't know.'

'Any idea at all?'

'Ummm. Well, when are *you* free?'

'When *you* are?'

We grin at one another and Isa groans. 'Goooooooodddddd.' She throws herself full length on the grass and writhes a bit. 'Just arrange it. Just *arrange* it. For the love of *Schubert*.'

Billy

For the love of Schubert?

That's a new one on me.

I drain most of my tea and put the cup down. There are some dregs in the bottom, so I frown and tip them out. They look a bit twiggy — God only knows what Isabel has put in there. She's a devil for experimenting with herbal concoctions.

'You've finished?' Isa squawks. She stops writhing and picks the cup up. 'You've *finished*?'

'Aye.'

'Lexie. Finish yours. Finish it! Quickly! And *arrange* something!'

'Oh, it's okay. I don't want to keep Billy if he needs to start the talk again.' Lexie pours what's left of her drink onto the grass and puts the cup down. Hopefully they'll forgive me for giving them another shower.' She points to the grass — or, I assume, to the people beneath the grass

'Nooooooo! Oh no!' Isa dives onto the cup and stares at the soggy grass. 'It's — I don't know — I . . .'

She looks up at me, worry flitting into her eyes, and I feel my face crease into that scowl again. I like to think of it as a quizzical expression, but I think I just look angry half the time when I pull this face. 'Isabel McCreadie. What is going on?' I hiss.

'I just . . . I just wanted you guys to enjoy a nice cup of tea.' She smiles at me, but I can tell it's fake as her skin looks all taut and stretched.

And then I get it.

'Ah. Isabel.' I lean closer to her and drop my voice to a whisper. *I get it now.* 'Are you matchmaking, by any chance?'

'Aye. Aye. That's it. I'm matchmaking, Uncle Billy. I am that.' She seems to deflate and draws the cups closer, then stacks them very carefully. My niece catches my eye again. 'Is that a problem?'

I close my eyes briefly in despair, then open them again. I look right at her. 'No, Isabel. It's not a problem. But you're causing a massive amount of fuss, and that is a problem. I've brought you out tonight as a favour, so please: respect that and behave.'

Her mouth turns upside down and I'm sure there's a wobble in the bottom lip, but she just screws the cups on top of the flask and won't look at me any more.

'Okay!' I say, loudly and overly-brightly. I stand up and look around. 'Is everybody ready for the next bit? We're going to talk about some of the famous residents of this beautiful resting place.'

There are nods and murmurs from the group, and they move closer to hear what I'm saying. I wait until everyone is pretty close, then lead them over to James Craig, who designed the first layout of Edinburgh New Town. He's a nice guy to start with, I think, before we get onto the grim deeds of Francis Charteris, notorious member of the Hellfire Club, and, of course, George Mackenzie's fabulous mausoleum. He shares that space with the murderer John Chieslie and the murderer's brother, Robert, and we always spend a long time there as inevitably people want to hear the ghost stories. I also like to chat about John's daughter, Rachel, otherwise known as Lady Grange, who was a bit wild in her time.

I think Rachel is great, but I doubt that idea was shared by her husband somehow, when you find out more about her. I'm not sure I'd want my wife threatening to run naked through the streets, or sleeping with a knife under her pillow just so I remember who her father is — but then again, her hubby was an unfaithful creature and had her kidnapped. Never a dull moment in that house, I reckon.

I dip my head and smile at the thought of Rachel and then look up again. I do a swift head count. Sixteen participants.

Sixteen?

There were only fifteen before. I suspect someone has tagged on. It often happens. *Never mind.*

'So here we go — James Craig . . .' I begin describing the deeds of that fine man, and my eyes rove around the group. I rest my gaze on different people as I talk. It makes them feel involved, and I generally get a smile and a nod in return. My gaze hovers longer on Lexie, and even I can hear my voice soften and feel my smile widen as I talk to her.

I think I've got it pretty bad.

I've liked girls before, of course I have. I didn't get to my early thirties without a bit of that. There may even have been a brief live-in girlfriend — well, she gradually moved in over a period of weeks until I realised she was taking over my Quayside Mills flat — but it was never going to work, to be honest. Vanessa was fluffy and blonde and giggly — everything, in fact, that Lexie isn't, come to think of it. Schubert didn't like Vanessa because she hated him anywhere near her, in case he shed fur on her designer gear (and, thinking about it, I've never seen him shed so much fur, either before or after that relationship broke up, which seems fairly suspicious to me) and Nessa despised her because she was, genuinely, called Vanessa, which my Nessa envied; her name is short for Agnes, which she hates, and she used to pretend it was Vanessa to impress people.

Vanessa was a secretary at the garage I used to work at when I sold cars for a living. It wasn't a great period in my life, to be honest. She wanted me dressed in suits all the time and to hold dinner parties for her posh girlfriends and their slick partners. I never fitted in.

I think the crunch came when my three brothers and Nessa all came to the flat for my birthday one year, and she couldn't stand the place being filled with loud McCreadies and cat hair.

We argued, and she said she was going back to her own place 'FOR-EVER!' Nessa helpfully packed her bags for her while we were still arguing, and I'm pretty sure Schubert's old grooming brush went in the case along with Vanessa's cream linen trousers and silk blouses, as I got a few vindictive texts afterwards which I deleted before happily blocking the woman and moving on to a new job without a backwards glance.

But I digress.

Today, in Greyfriars Kirkyard, of all places, my attention is held by a girl with long, multi-coloured hair, a grungy coat and body piercings.

I grin — I can't help it — and she grins back.

I'd like to say we shared a moment. But then I hear something which sends all my senses into overdrive — and I mean all of them.

'For the love of *Odin*!'

I look over Lexie's shoulder, and there's a girl there. She appears to be absolutely furious and her hands are balled into fists. She's wearing a big, long, flouncy tartan skirt, a grubby white blouse and a tightly laced corset thing. Her hair is as wild and as curly as my sister's, but it's a dirty blonde colour and looks as if it could do with a wash and a comb through it.

She stomps around from behind Lexie, who doesn't even flinch. Then she stands in front of her, looking straight at me. 'Whae did it? Whae *did* it? You?' She points a dirt-stained finger, tipped with a broken, stubby nail at me. Her voice is pure Scottish with a lilt in it that's hard to place.

Nobody else is taking any notice of her at all, and the group is all just standing there expectantly, waiting for me to continue my stories.

I open my mouth to respond, then she flaps her hand around a bit, dismissing a potential response from me and glares at us all, before turning her back on me. 'You! You. It's *you*, aye?' She marches over to Isabel, who's standing at the edge of the group and staring back at the girl, her eyes like saucers.

'Now wait a minute!' I say.

The group looks at me startled, and then I feel the colour drain from my face as the tartan-clad girl walks straight through the crowd of paying guests and stands in front of Isabel. She's only about the same height as my niece, and Isa is, to give her her due, pulling herself up to her full height and putting her own hands on her hips and facing Tartan-Girl down.

But I can't actually respond, because when I say the tartan-clad girl walked through the crowd, she did exactly that. She walked through them.

Through them.

As if she was simply walking through mist without substance.

Or as if she *was* the mist without substance.

Dear God.

This casts a whole new light on everything . . .

4

Lexie

Billy has just stopped dead. He's gawping at nothing in particular, and I begin to wonder whether he's thinking about teatime tomorrow. Maybe he's inwardly reminding himself that he needs to get something out of the freezer to defrost?

That's the sort of thing that would cause me to gape into thin air, but I'd more than likely be thinking about cake.

Or maybe he's seen an actual ghost?

Which is unlikely.

There's a sort of scuffle behind me, and I shiver as one of those unpredictable Scottish winds blows past me. Then Isabel mutters something like, 'Don't you dare say that!' and stomps behind a mausoleum.

I turn back to Billy, wondering what on earth she's taken such umbrage to, and his eyes are fixed on the thing as well. I glance over, just in case I'm missing something as his face has gone all hard and a muscle is twitching in his jaw. I see the edge of a long, filthy tartan skirt just disappearing around the corner of the mausoleum. *Curious*. I wonder if this is one of those tours where live actors leap out at you. They did that at the Dracula Experience in Whitby when I was there. I'm afraid I laughed in the chap's face and he skulked off. I don't scare easily. I'm too practical for that.

'Okay!' Billy says suddenly, over-brightly, and he pastes a sickly sort of smile on his face and turns back to face us all. 'So, the guy we're going to meet *here* is famous for the beautiful landscape at the heart of this fabulous town . . . '

And he prattles on about an archi-tect called James Craig for a little while. Apparently, this good gentleman can be found under a slab at our feet that wasn't put there until the 1930s. It seems they banned monuments until the nineteenth century, and this poor guy died in 1795.

It's fascinating stuff, but Billy appears to have part of his mind elsewhere. His eyes are roving around all over the place but maybe I'm the only one who's noticing, as I am *very* focused on those eyes. I wonder if Isabel is off to plan something with the actress . . . or perhaps she's just a bit bored. When I was a teenager, I couldn't concentrate on any one thing for too long without feeling bored, so it doesn't surprise me if she's disappeared to text her mates or watch YouTube videos.

All too soon, for me, we complete our tour of the churchyard and everyone tells Billy how much they've enjoyed it. The tartan-skirted actress still hasn't popped out at us. Perhaps she's from a different tour and Isa is telling her to back off? It wouldn't surprise me, from what I've seen of Isa.

Billy nods and smiles and shakes hands with the group of people, murmuring pleasantries until they all peel away and go their separate ways. I sort of hovered at the back whilst that was going on, so now I'm left alone with him, and I feel a little awkward and obvious. I shrug my backpack further onto my shoulders and he comes across to me, still looking a bit spaced out.

'Thank you,' I say. 'That was a good tour.'

'I'm the best in the business.' Then, all in a rush: 'Have you see Isa? At all? Anywhere?' His eyes rove around again, and he looks quite pale for some reason.

'She went behind that.' I point at the tomb, although I realise it's a fair way away now, across the other side of the churchyard.

'Was she on her own?' His voice is a bit clipped and short, and slightly angry.

I'm a bit stunned and involuntarily step backwards. 'Yes.' I answer equally shortly. 'Unless you count the woman in the tartan skirt. I thought she was one of your lot. But she hasn't jumped out at us, so maybe not.'

'Shit.'

Okay. Well I wasn't expecting that. Ex-girlfriend, maybe? Encroaching on his territory? It's possible.

One thing's for certain, I'm clearly not

going to be invited to have a fun night with Billy McCreadie if he's in that sort of mood, am I? So much for the fantasies I was weaving about him and his cutlass. So much for that idea that I would purr to him, 'Oh, take me back somewhere and keep telling me these stories. You're soooooo interesting ...' But then I'm not a one for purring, to be honest.

But someone clearly is.

'Mow wow?' The noise comes from behind a gravestone and is followed by a large black cat, picking his way across the grass. He's looking left and right, almost nodding to the residents of the cemetery, as if he's acknowledging them all beneath his four paws. His greeting was slightly muffled, but that's probably because he has a purple lead in his mouth. It seems he's taking himself for a walk.

'Schubert?' The name on Billy's lips sounds superfluous — it is, of course, Schubert.

'Mow wow.' He comes to stand between us and studies us, then his gaze drifts off to the mausoleum Isa was behind, and his ears prick up. He freezes and looks quizzical, even to the point of dropping his lead. 'Mow wow!' He shoots off to the structure and, quite soon, Isa comes out from behind it, her face all closed up.

'Isabel McCreadie.' Billy stares at her. 'Have you something to say?'

She drops her head and mutters something that sounds like 'no'.

'Isa! Good God, you have to say *something*!' Billy tugs the ribbon out of his ponytail and runs his hands through his hair. I feel my jaw slackening. I have seriously always loved a man with long hair, and as I watch it flop over his shoulders and see him shake it back, all whilst glaring at his niece, I feel quite weak at the knees.

'Okay,' I say quickly, or rather I squeak quickly in a high-pitched fashion. 'Cool. I'll be off. I guess you have to take Isabel home now.' I smile, and the smile definitely feels fake, as if I'm stretching it across my face and I don't really mean

86

it. 'Like I say, great tour. Really great. I'll head to the library first thing Monday. Look some of these guys up. Genealogy, you know.' I laugh, even more fakely. 'Maybe I'll be related to one of them. Okay. Great tour. Goodnight. Goodnight, Isa. Goodnight, Schubert. Say goodnight to your . . . friend . . . as well. Right. Goodnight all.'

Nobody answers me, except the cat, and I melt away into the shadows which are forming around the cemetery. I shiver and look back over my shoulder. I have the funniest feeling that somebody is watching me, but there's nobody there. Of course there isn't.

Billy has his hands on his hips, and Isa is mirroring him. They are leaning towards one another as if they are preparing for an argument, and Schubert has sat down between them, looking up from one to the other. Then he, too, runs off in the direction he's come from, and that's it. There's not another living soul in that place.

And I don't believe in ghosts.

'So, *this* is awkward,' Nessa says. She's standing on her doorstep when I get back to her house, hands on hips. It seems to be the McCreadie stance this evening. Isa and I were just doing the same thing in the churchyard, and, when we eventually stopped yelling at one another and I looked up, Lexie had vanished.

Instead of Lexie, there was this Tartan-Girl again. She was leaning against a tombstone, inspecting her fingernails and looking bored, as if she'd heard the same thing over and over again.

She was dripping now, a pool of water around her feet, but she seemed unconcerned and only dragged herself away from the thing when I demanded we go back to Nessa's. She followed us as far as the gates, then stopped.

'Oh, thank *you*, my pet!' I heard her shriek as we stepped out onto the path. 'A bloody *binding* spell! Yon wee anes these days . . . !' She was still yelling at us and throwing in a select choice of strange Nordic-sounding words as we left. I practically dragged my niece along the road back to Nessa's.

'Nessa, I'm not speaking to your niece tonight. I'm just not,' I growl at my sister. Nessa is pretty much rocking the Valkyrie look, blocking the entrance to her house, but Isa still manages to slip past her.

'She's from Orkney. She's from *Orkney*!' Isa is muttering, as if that's a crime and it was Tartan-Girl's fault that she was in the middle of Greyfriars Kirkyard and not back on Orkney.

'I don't care where she's bloody from!' I explode as Isabel stalks into Nessa's house and tosses the clipboard down with a clatter. *My clipboard. Mine.* Nessa stands back to let me get past, realising, perhaps, that I'm an extremely angry person at the moment. 'All I care about is why she appeared in the middle of our tour!' It's pointless reminding myself that I'm the adult again, because I don't think I'm going to stop shouting until I get answers.

'Isabel is *your* niece as well,' says Nessa piously. 'But I do think Isa needs to explain herself.' She follows us in. 'Schubert has told me the story as he sees it. Isa's new friend is called Mhairi and, as Isa correctly says, Mhairi is from Orkney.'

'She's no' my *friend*!' bellows Isabel and punches a cushion.

'Mow wow?' Schubert slopes up beside Nessa and looks up at her quizzically. He's sucking up and trying to look innocent, any fool can see that. I think Isabel is going to implode any moment as we're all ignoring her; if there's anything guaranteed to make Isa fizz with temper it's being ignored. 'No, darling,' Nessa says to Schubert gently. 'Isa's quite right. Her name is pronounced *Vaa-ree*. You can't just call her Mary. That's not her name.'

'Mow wow.' The cat slinks off and I stare at him, speechless. *I. Can't. Even . . .*

'So. Your question, William, about *why* Isabel's friend appeared is quite valid,' Nessa continues as if everything is completely normal and ushers me further inside. I blink — this is surreal. It is totally surreal. 'And I think we do need Isa to explain what she did,' she adds serenely.

'It's not *fair*!' Isa yells and dashes upstairs. She knows she's rumbled. Two floors above us, I can hear a door slam faintly. That's her locked away until tomorrow then. Or until she's hungry, I guess.

'She said,' I say, almost choking on the words, because *seriously*? 'She — Mhairi — ' My voice cracks a little on her name, because she is definitely a ghost, dammit, ' — said something about a binding spell.' I close my eyes and hope that nobody has a listening device in this house, because they'd never believe the conversation. Never in a million years.

'Oh.' Nessa stares at me, unblinking. 'That's not good.'

'Nessa — Isa was in your basement — '

'My Witchy Consultancy.'

' — your Witchy Consultancy, before

we left. She brought a flask with her. With tea in it. For us to drink.' I stare at Nessa as the pieces suddenly fall into place. 'Was it that? Was it the tea? The tea in the bloody flask?'

'It sounds likely,' Nessa says carefully. She pulls a face. 'I did think she could be trusted down there. But I see she may be beyond the rosewater and lavender ointment stage. Hmmm.' She sits down on the bottom stair and puts her chin in her hands. 'Hmmmm.'

"Hmmm' isn't good enough! Move over.' Nessa obligingly shuffles over, and I sit next to her, mirroring her position. 'What can we do?'

'Well, you're the one who sees ghosts more than I do,' says Nessa. 'It's your call.'

Because, this you have it, is my Deep, Dark Secret.

I see ghosts.

I always have done.

It's just that I'm kind of used to the ones I see, and there's been nobody new for a while. The friends I mentioned in

Edinburgh's oldest pub? Well, there's not a corporeal one amongst them.

Seeing Mhairi was a bit of a shock to the old system. I've learned to tune them out and would never willingly summon any of them; so to see that my niece has managed to do that, by whatever method, has upset and annoyed me more than I thought possible.

Rest in Peace: that's what we all deserve, isn't it? Why knowingly disturb someone? If it's their choice to come back to see you, that's different. But nobody wants to be dragged back out of the grave.

So, I can understand Mhairi's frustration and anger — and, also, what the hell is a girl from Orkney, dressed in the height of Jacobite fashion, doing in the twenty-first century, haunting a graveyard?

'I've never had them yell at me and swear in weird languages,' I say. Nessa has, to my knowledge, only seen our Great Great Grandmother Agnes, who she was named after. She's not experienced anyone like Mhairi. I mean,

Rachel — Lady Grange — is hot-headed enough, but she has cause and we get on fine. As for James Craig, he's a pleasant chap but keeps himself to himself when there's a group in the graveyard. He says he's a bit worried his creditors will come and ask for some cash if he socialises too much, which is understandable.

But Mhairi? Where the hell does she fit in?

I wrack my brains trying to think of a 'Mhairi' in the cemetery, and there aren't any gravestones that spring to mind that may be hers.

'What was Isa trying to do? Was it anything to do with that young lady who looked after Schubert?'

'Yes.' I sigh. 'She said she was match-making. She made us both drink some tea.'

'Ahh.' Nessa nods. 'Did any of it end up on the ground?' She drops her voice to a theatrical whisper. 'In the *graves*? Soaking into the *graves*? The graves *beneath your feet*?'

'There's no need to keep repeating yourself, Nessa!' I snap.

'I'm just saying. *The gr —*'

'Agnes!' It's my older brother voice, and she finally shuts her mouth and purses her lips together.

'Fine,' she mutters when she's un-pursed them. I knew she wouldn't be able to stay quiet for long. 'I'm just saying, depending on what she used and what she said, and who was . . . beneath your feet — ' she casts a sly glance at me, but I can't be bothered to argue with her ' — she might have caused a wee bit of mischief.'

'But she didn't go digging up anything, and all we did was drink the sodding tea, and . . .' My voice trails off as I remember. *Oh, shit.* 'Apart from the bits that got tipped out onto the ground.'

I look at Nessa, who puts that holier-than-thou face on again. 'On the ground. So, it soaked into the — '

'Shut up!'

' — grass.' She looks at me even more slyly. 'It soaked into the *grass*. What if your friend was under there? We've already established the possibility of a binding

95

spell. It's easy to make mistakes with the ingredients. A bit too much of one of them and — *whoops*. That could well be it.' She drums her fingertips thoughtfully on her chin and nods. 'Yes. That makes sense. If she's put too much of one thing in and not enough of another, and then got her words mixed up . . .'

I recall that Isa was muttering something as she was pouring the liquid into the cups, and I feel sick. *She has, hasn't she? She's done a spell.*

'Yes. If she's done *that*,' continues my sister, 'then you'll be more bound to one another than matched. Hmm. Yes. That's it, then. Good.' She bounces to her feet and starts walking away.

'Nessa!' I scramble up and hurry after her. 'What can we do to un-bind us then? I'm pretty sure that Orkney lass doesn't want to be stuck in an Edinburgh cemetery for the rest of her afterlife.'

'I'm pretty sure she doesn't.'

'Mow wow.' Schubert is clearly in agreement. But then he hasn't finished yet. 'Mow wow,' he says and climbs heavily onto the table where Nessa has put three glasses and is unscrewing the lid from a wine bottle.

Nessa nods at him and ruffles his fur. 'Quite right, my darling. Then she calls, 'Ewan! There's wine on the go!' She looks at me and hands me a glass. 'You can stay for one with us as you've had a trauma, but I'm afraid I'm not going to be allowing you to stay beyond that. I have entertaining to do with Ewan. You, on the other hand, have to go home and Think about what *you* need to do.'

'Think about what I need to do?' I stare at her. Again, she's implied that capital letter at the beginning of 'think'. How does she do that? I also cringe inwardly, thinking of how my baby sister is going to be 'entertaining' Ewan once Maggie and Isabel are safely stashed away.

My family are like bloody rabbits.

'Yes.' Nessa is emphatic. 'What reason would a girl from up *there* — ' she points with her glass to in vague north-easterly direction ' — be doing *here*? How can you find out her story?'

'I have no idea.' I take a slug of wine as if it's a vodka shot.

'You need to research it. That's what you need to do. Talk to people.' She waves her glass around. 'Listen to people. *Research* it.'

'Research it.' I nod mutely and drain the glass. 'Fine. I'll go. See you soon. Thanks for nothing.'

'You're welcome.' She smiles at me. 'After all, it's not *me* who needs to sort it out. It's *you*. I can only suggest the tools necessary for the job.'

'Oh, shut up, Agnes.' But the fight has gone out of me. I relent and give her a quick hug, because I do love her really, and then I head out of the house before she can say anything else that's going to knot my brain up even further.

Research it? I think I need to crack open another bottle of wine at home and Think about it.

'Oh! Hey Billy.' Ewan appears in the hallway as I'm heading out of the house. He must have been lurking upstairs, doing his writing or whatever. Or, more than likely, on a conference call to somewhere exotic. 'I was just on a conference call. Skype. Hollywood.' He rakes his hand through his short hair and grins almost apologetically. He flushes. 'Sorry. I would have come down earlier . . . '

'No, it's fine. Aye. Enjoy your evening.' I nod. 'She's in there.' I gesture towards the kitchen where I left Nessa. 'Isa's upstairs in a huff. She'll not be back down tonight. And I'm assuming Mags is stashed somewhere as well, so . . . aye. Have fun.'

Ewan flushes even more, and I know I really need to get out of here.

Rabbits. All rabbits.

I nod again and make to hurry out of the door.

'Oh! Pop around for a cuppa tomorrow at tea time,' says Ewan, and I think I feel pity emanating from him. 'It'll be nice to see you properly.'

'Hmmmphhh.' I make a non-committal sort of noise as I leave. I don't need pity cuppas, I really don't.

I need to Think.

5

Billy

I've Thought, and there's only one thing I can Think of. I need to go and do some research as my sister says. I can't believe it took me a bottle of red wine to Think of that one.

Halfway down a second bottle, it seemed like a bloody good idea — but this morning I regretted it all, as I had a slight hangover and half a bottle of wine left over.

But it wasn't enough to stop me from going to Nessa's for tea. Ewan texted me earlier, and so I figured that he really must want to see me, for some reason.

I'm heading up her street, shades on, walking the hangover off, and then I see my parents' car there, along with Scotty's and Hugo's. I hurry up a bit, my stomach churning as it's not often we're all together. I start to think something bad has happened to Nessa, or perhaps even Schubert, and Alfie throws the door open to me just before I knock.

'Afternoon, Bono. You've been summoned too?' He frowns. I step inside, not asking how he knew I was on the steps. Or why he's calling me Bono. Or which one of our other brothers encouraged him to do that.

'Eff off. Is everything okay?' I look around the hallway and am ridiculously pleased when Schubert smarms up to me and rubs against my leg.

'Mow wow,' Schubert says and slips out of the house. He flops down the steps, and Alfie shakes his head at the Beast's retreating bum before shutting the door.

'I think so. Did you get a text from Ewan?'

'I did.'

'Me too,' says Scott, joining us. 'Has anyone seen Liza or Isa?'

'I here, Daddy,' says a little voice from around our ankles, and Scott ducks down and picks up Mags. He balances her on his shoulders and she giggles.

101

Scott, however, is still frowning and looking around for his other girls.

Hugo appears from one of the rooms leading off the hallway, holding his mobile phone out. 'Isla's gone too. I wanted to show you all the scan photos, but she says to hang on for a few minutes until she comes back. But I don't know where she is.'

'Afternoon, guys.' Ewan appears from another door. We're still all stood in the hallway, and Maggie is the only one who's currently taller than her Uncle Ewan.

She leans over and pats him. 'Ahhh,' she says, then leans down and kisses his head.

'Maggie May. You've grown!' says Ewan and the toddler giggles.

Everyone seems in a good mood, apart from my abandoned brothers. I can hear Nessa laughing at something in the lounge, accompanied by the rumbling tones of Dad and the gossipy voice of Mum, so there's nothing wrong there either.

We stare at one another in consternation, and Alfie shrugs. 'I'm sure it will all become clear,' he says, and we all shrug again in unison before heading into the lounge.

'Yay! You're all here!' Nessa smiles around at us and dispenses hugs. 'It's so lovely to see you all together. How nice that Ewan invited you all. I — oh. Schubert. He's outside isn't he? I'd best go and open the door for him.'

She jumps off the chair and dashes to the hallway.

'Ummmm — you might want to follow her,' says Ewan, and his cheeks are redder than ever. He's like a shambling buffoon and totally on edge. We all stare at him and at one another.

And then Alfie speaks. 'Oh, God. Oh God. I know what's coming . . .' He looks at us, pale-faced and terrified. And, knowing Alfie, it's not surprising that he knows what's coming, because he often does — but it is surprising that he looks so ghastly. 'Take cover, guys,' he mutters. 'I mean it.'

I'm out for a stroll and I've found a really nice part of the New Town. I wonder idly whether James Craig was responsible for this bit, and then something runs at me, then bounces off me weightily and disappears up a side street.

The something is a large black cat. I'd even go so far as to say it's the largest black cat I've seen, equivalent only to — 'Schubert!' I hurry after him, wondering what he's doing here.

'Mow wow!' He pauses in his fast waddling, because that's what his run equates to really, and looks at me brightly.

'Schubert!' I dash after him, my laptop bag bouncing across my body. 'What are doing out here? Oh!' I draw up short in front of two women, one red-haired and one fair-haired, who have cornered Schubert.

Having said that, when I look again, I think Schubert has cornered them.

'Oh! Hi, Lexie.' A voice yells up the side street at me, and I turn to see Isabel standing there with her mobile phone in her hand. 'You're just in time. Ummm — have you spoken to Uncle Billy today?' Her cheeks flush pink for some reason.

'Hi, Isa.' I'm a bit taken aback to see her there. 'No. I haven't. Should I have done?'

'Nope. You didn't speak to him last night either, did you? After the tour?'

'No.' It's my turn to blush. 'Not really.'

'Okay.' She nods. Then she obviously thinks that she needs to do some introductions. She waves her hand in the direction of the two women. 'That's my mum. That's my auntie.'

The women look up and attempt to smile, although they seem distracted by Schubert, who is now lying flat on the ground and moaning about something.

'Lexie? Hi. I'm Liza,' says the redhead. 'Isa's my daughter, for my sins. This is Isla.' She nods to the fair-haired woman who is now sitting on the ground with Schubert's head in her lap. 'Isabel mentioned that she'd met you again last night. You were with Billy, weren't you? On the tour. She said you'd looked after Schubert for him as well the other day. Sorry — he's not being the best of boys today — are you, Schubert? I think you're being a little bit difficult, and you've got an important job to do.'

I stare at the cat who moans pathetically. 'He just sort of bounced off me in the street.' I wave towards the main road. 'He seemed as if he was in quite a hurry. Is he not being cooperative?'

'Not very. I don't think he understands what we need to do.'

'I think we should just tell him,' pipes up Isa. 'Don't give in to him. He knows full well what to do. He's just attention-seeking.'

There's a snort from Liza. 'And we all know what attention-seeking is, don't we?'

'Aye, it's dressing in clothes that were made for a younger person,' responds Isabel with a sniff.

'Shut up, child,' says Liza mildly, then looks at Schubert again. 'Oh come on,

Schubert. We're doing this for Nessa. You know what's happening. Ewan's already spoken to you.'

'Be a good boy,' says the blonde — Isla. 'You know we like to get dressed up, don't we? You *know* you're my best boy.'

'Mow wow?' He looks up at her.

'Yes, Opal is a girl cat. So, you're definitely my best boy. Be good.'

I look at the cat and see a box lying beside him. It's a box that looks as if it's from a jewellers. There's a purple ribbon attached to it. Schubert eyes the box, huffs and puffs a little, then finally sits up nice and straight.

'Good boy!' Isla ties the ribbon around where his neck should realistically be. 'Very good boy. Now you know exactly what to do, don't you?'

'Mow w — '

'In a minute!' cries Isabel. 'I need to get into position. Hang around, Lexie, this is gonna be F-U-N.'

'O-M-G,' mutters Liza and stands up. 'Right. Give us a moment, then.' She waits until Isa has disappeared around the corner and shrugs her shoulders helplessly. 'Schubert, you know what you have to do.'

'Mow wow,' he replies, quite obligingly, I think, and then he stands up quite proudly and begins to mince along the pavement.

There's no other word for it. I watch him, fascinated, as he wiggles along, and I feel a smile twitch at my lips. 'Where's he going?'

'Nessa and Ewan's house.' Isla nods after him. 'All the family are there, so I hope this works out well.'

'Me too,' says Liza. 'Ewan's planned it out the best way he can. Come on. Let's go and watch.' She looks over at me and smiles. 'Welcome to the madhouse. Life is never dull when you're with the McCreadies.'

'Oh, but . . . '

The women shake their heads in unison and grin. '*He* likes you.' Isla points to the cat. 'You're one of us now.'

'No denying it.' Liza smiles at me again. 'Come on. Let's watch.'

Then, somehow, I'm ushered out into the street and we follow Schubert as he continues to mince his way along.

We all stop, and even as I'm questioning how on earth I got to this point and wondering at the workings of Fate, the cat makes his way up a set of stone steps to a big, old town house. As he gets to the door, it flings open. Isa is standing filming it on her mobile, and I can see her grinning like mad.

Then there's a pause, and then the loudest shriek of delight I've ever heard as a pretty, dark-haired girl comes to the door: 'Schubert! There you are — what? What's that?'

'Mow wow. Mow wow. Mow wow.'

Another pause. 'What? *Really? Oh Schubert!*' She dips down and unties the ribbon and opens the box. Her eyes widen and she turns to look inside, a huge smile on her face. 'Ewan! Oh *Ewan*. How clever. Oh, how clever. Oh *Ewan*, I love *you*. And I love you, Schubert. I do, I do, I do! Yes! I love you *both* and yes, *I will*. The answer is yes! Oh *Ewan*! Oh

Schubert!' Then another pause, followed by the same female voice from the doorstep going, 'Alfie. Alfie, as my twin, will you help organise the wedding? *Will* you?'

'Hell no, Nessa. No, no I won't,' a male voice responds from inside the house.

'Oh, you will, you will . . . ' and the voices grow fainter as the people move indoors and the three of us are left standing on the pavement.

'I think that was a 'yes'.' Isla and Liza high-five each other, and Isa comes running over.

'I got it, I got it all. #Schubertthecat #engagement #catsofinstagram. Get in!' She punches the air and grins at me.

I grin back, but it's a wavery grin as my attention is suddenly arrested by the next person at the door. It's a man who is all too familiar and, as he peers outside, he starts when he sees me. He pushes his sunglasses onto the top of his head and our eyes lock and everything else disappears. He steps outside.

Liza touches my sleeve gently. 'See you soon, no doubt. Come on, Isabel.

Let's join in the celebrations. I think your Uncle Billy wants to chat to Lexie here.' Then she takes Isa's hand and propels her towards the house, and I'm vaguely aware of the three of them sidestepping Billy and disappearing inside. Isa, I notice, ducks her head and slips past him quicker than any of the others, but I don't dwell on why this could be as I'm more concerned with the man heading towards me, his eyes never leaving mine.

'Lexie.' His voice is warm and slightly uncertain. He clears his throat. 'That was fun, wasn't it? And entirely unexpected, I think, from all of us. I knew something was going on, though — but I'm pleased it was that rather than anything else. I'm even more pleased that I've seen you. You see, I need to do some research, and I think you mentioned that you'd be in the library tomorrow morning? Am I right?'

I nod, speechless, and he nods back.

'Good.' He grins and I can't help grinning back. 'I'll see you there then. Tomorrow? Ten o'clock?'

I find my voice. 'Ten o'clock sounds good to me.'

'Good. Ummm . . . do you want to come in? Help us celebrate?'

The thought is tempting, but I shake my head. 'No. No, that's family time, that is. You go on in. I'll see you tomorrow.'

'Okay. If you're sure.'

'I'm sure.' I'm not really. I do want to go in, mainly just to be near Billy — but I know that wouldn't really be polite, so I shake my head resolutely. 'No. Like I say, it's family time. See you at ten.'

'See you at ten. And . . . umm, I probably need to explain a couple of things to you as well.'

'Okay.' I look at him in surprise. 'Nothing bad?'

'Nothing bad. Just what I need to research. And why.' A frown scuttles across his face but vanishes almost immediately, and he smiles again. 'Tomorrow then. Ten. Yes?'

'Yes. Ten.'

'See you then.'

For a moment, I think that he's about

112

to kiss me — then I pull myself out of the little fantasy I've just woven together on the spot and step back. 'See you tomorrow. Enjoy your night — oh, and congratulations. It's your sister, yes?'

'Yup. My sister.'

'Cool. Bye then.' I nod and stuff my hands in my pocket.

'Bye then.' He nods back, and we do an awkward little dance thing. I think it's actually best if I turn around and head back the way I've come, leaving the path clear for him to go back to the house, so as not to enter into an even more awkward 'walking together' situation.

So, that's exactly what I do. I turn on my heel, give him another nod and smile, and hurry back the way I've come.

But you know what? I really can't wait until tomorrow at ten.

Billy

That was inspired. That was truly inspired.

The library. Of *course*, the library. Where else would I go to research Mhairi Tartan-Girl? And who else would I go with, if not a genealogist? The library is exactly where I'm heading now, even though I find myself taking a ridiculously circuitous route to get there, via Greyfriars of all places.

Of course, the fact that Lexie's a stunner isn't even part of the equation — but honestly, I can't stop smiling to myself when I think of how I looked outside and there she was with Isla and Liza and Isabel, of all people.

They said that Schubert had sort of barrelled off her and she'd come up the side street after him — but how cool that she happened to be passing at that particular time, at that particular moment . . .

'Aye, it's alreet for some, being on *time* for suchlike.' The round, northerly tones assault my eardrums as I jump and Mhairi appears from behind a damn mausoleum again. I seriously do *not* know why I chose to walk past

Greyfriars today . . .

Mhairi suddenly zooms over to the gates and peers at me angrily through the bars. 'Where's the wee ane? Yon *felkyo*. She needs to get me out of — ' she pokes her finger at nothing in particular, at everything around her ' — *here*.'

Her voice is almost musical, and the 'r' rolls beautifully as Mhairi says the word 'here', but I haven't got time to compliment her on her accent or ask her what the hell '*felkyo*' means. Instead, I turn on her and stare at her furious little face. It strikes me that she'd be really pretty if she wasn't screwing her face up like she was chewing a wasp. 'Mhairi. What's your surname?'

She's taken aback slightly and zooms backwards then forwards again. 'My surname?'

'Yes. Your last name.'

'I ken whit a surname is!' She glares at me. 'I just dinnae ken why ye need it.'

'So we can help you.' I can't help it. I hiss, equally angrily back at her, then look around me. I'm going to look crazy if anyone is following me. 'I'm coming in,' I tell her. 'Wait there.'

'*Oho*! No' like I can do much else, is it?' she mutters and rattles the gates a bit. I ignore her and slip into the cemetery. 'And I'm *not* telling you my name.' She scuttles after me and I ignore her. I'm too used to Nessa to be bothered by her pettiness.

I walk nonchalantly towards James Craig, then take a slight diversion towards Henry Siddons, the actor. I'm sure he knew a bit about keeping his cool in stressful situations and, as he wrote a play about a ghost, he's a kindred spirit, pardon the pun, and won't stand any extra nonsense from this girl.

Mhairi darts to and fro, grumbling at intervals as she powers through — yes through — the big, upright tombstones, keeping pace with me. She's still not spilling her name, though.

'Surname, Mhairi, please,' I say, putting on a bored voice and leaning against Henry's tomb. 'Unless you don't *want* us to be able to find out anything about you, that is. Anything that might help you.'

'Smith.' She glares at me. 'It's *Smith*.' Then her eyes dart away from me, and I just know she's lying.

'It's not Smith. What is it?'

'Brown.' She looks up at the sky.

'Nope.'

'Thomson?' She picks at that finger-nail again.

'Liar.'

'Siddons.'

'*Absolutely* a liar. You've just read that off this stone.'

'Have not.'

'Have so. Okay. Fine. Stay here. I don't really care.' I push myself away from Henry and make as if to leave, but she swears again and appears in front of me.

'Clouston. It's Clouston, aye?' She glowers up at me. 'It's not a common name. They can *find* me if they know it . . . and I widnae be welcomed back, I *widnae*. But aye, aye, Bonnie Prince Charlie would help me if he could, he *would*. Aye, after all we did for him . . .'

She's off on one again, stomping and swearing, and she's still going strong after several minutes have passed.

I'm confused, but I do believe her this time as there's a hint of trepidation as well as defiance in her eyes. Indeed, I am truly baffled. Not only is a ghost lying to me about her surname, but why on earth — or anywhere else for that matter — would she be so concerned about her name being discovered? And why would she be unwelcome?

'Mhairi Clouston. From Orkney. About 1745 — or thereabouts?'

'Argh!' She makes the sign of warding off evil at me, a witch-sign, no less, and backs away. 'How d'ye ken a' that?'

I roll my eyes heavenwards — where, all things being equal, my companion should be — and head away from Henry.

Then I stop and face her again. 'You told Isabel, the girl you were speaking to. And I guessed the date from your clothes. And Bonnie Prince Charlie.'

'Oh! Aye. Aye. That's right.' Mhairi relaxes a bit and sits down on the edge of a mortsafe we've just arrived at. She flicks a gaze at the words written on it; the Latin for 'Not all of me will die'.

I vaguely wonder how she's actually sitting on the iron railing when she might have been expected to just fall through it, but then I think I don't need to know that, really.

Her face softens a bit as she studies the words, then she points at the phrase. 'I believe that. I know what it means, and I believe it. I heard tell what it meant . . .' Her voice trails off, then she looks back at me and her face hardens again. 'So. Any ideas? I need to be away from here. I dinnae need to be *bound*.'

'Are you bound to the ground . . . here?' I don't want to say grave or cemetery, as that's a wee bit insensitive.

'You tell me.' She glares at me. 'That wee ane caused it.' She waves her hand around. 'Got it all wrong, she did. All wrong.' She jumps to her feet and I notice there's water running off her hair and dripping off her skirt again. Mhairi gestures to her hair and scowls.

'This happens when I get worried or sad. I *drip*. All I wanted was to — ' She stops suddenly, then shakes her head and water droplets fly off her matted curls. 'No. I'm no' sayin'. You have to get me out of here. *Out!*'

She *whooshes* right up to me, right into my face, then vanishes in a swirl of tartan, leaving nothing but a brief rainbow behind as the sun slices through the space she and her water recently inhabited.

'But it would help me to know a bit more!' I say, looking around me. But she's gone.

Giving up, I check my watch. If I run, I'll still make it to meet Lexie on time — and at least I've got a bit to go on now. Mhairi Clouston from Orkney, circa 1745. It can't be that hard to find her — can it?

6

Lexie

Billy is a few minutes late. I've already got my laptop set up, a clean page open in my fancy notebook and a nice pen, all uncapped and ready for use. The pen I've chosen today writes in sea-blue ink and the notebook pages are edged with mint-green, so it should be a weird and wonderful combination — a sort of mermaid colour scheme. I'm looking forward to seeing what the page turns out like.

Just for good measure, I draw a little conch shell and a treasure chest in the bottom corner of my page and smile. I'm hoping to find out about one of my ancestors who has links up here, and a treasure chest is a good one to play with because there are indications he was a smuggler —

'God, I'm sorry!' Billy flies across the room to me, his hair pulled loosely back

121

again, his eyes wide and his face apologetic. 'I got held up.'

I smile at him. 'No worries. I was just setting up. Here, I kept you a seat.' I gesture to the chair next to me and move my bag off it. 'I wasn't sure how busy the library would be, so I got prepared.'

'Thanks.' He smiles gratefully and sits down. It might have felt weird, but it doesn't. Genealogy is a bit of a lonesome occupation at times, but oddly I feel quite relaxed whenever I'm going to start on a session, and Billy being a little late isn't going to spoil anything.

'I knew you'd turn up eventually,' I tell him, just so he knows it's all cool. 'Is there anything in particular you want to look at? Do you want to chat about anything before you start? Need any help with resources? Sorry . . . ' I grin. 'I feel like I'm at work — it's too easy to slip into that mindset when I'm somewhere like this.'

'Well . . . actually. Yes.' He looks at me and it almost seems like he's scared to say what he needs help with. 'There's a girl, you see . . . '

'Oh.' I feel a little deflated. Is he wanting to stalk someone to track their whereabouts? Or check up on an ex? The tartan one from the kirkyard, perhaps. 'I'm not sure how up to date the resources are in here for that sort of thing. Not entirely sure it's legal, anyway — '

'Oh! No — nothing like that.' He grins, looking right into my eyes. 'She's from 1745. Ish. I only know a couple of facts about her. I was hoping you'd help me dig.'

'Oh!' *That's better. That's much better.* 'Is she part of your family? Someone you know a little about and want to know more about?'

'Aye. Sort of. She has . . . ummm . . . *links* with my family.' He smiles again, and his voice is warm and he's looking right at me, making my stomach do that wibbly thing.

'O-kay.' I clear my throat and tear my gaze away from his, pretending to look efficient and in control as I draw my laptop nearer. 'What's her name?'

'Vaaree Clouston. Only it's spelled M-h-a-i-r-i.'

'So, a bit like Mary? It's a pretty name, isn't it?'

'It is.'

'And where does she come from?' My fingers hover over the keyboard expectantly.

'Orkney.'

'Date?'

'About 1745.' He shrugs. 'Give or take. I know she has Jacobite leanings, and her clothes are from that era . . .'

I smile as I type the details into my laptop. 'You talk as if she's real. I'm guessing you saw a picture of her, to know about her clothes and things?'

'You could say that.' He doesn't expand, but I'm very conscious of him leaning closer towards me and eyeing up my screen. 'Why isn't there anything coming up for her?' He looks at me in consternation. 'I thought these systems were all whistles and bells.'

'They are, but there may not be many records of Orkney at that time. It's a good starting point and we expand the search from there. Look. I'll show you where you might be able to find some info out, and there are other places we can try — other libraries. I know, for instance, that there was a guy who wrote quite a lot about the place, but it was well before the dates you want. Again, it's a starting point.'

'Oh?' Billy looks interested, so I barrel on.

'There are records of a guy called Jo Ben who travelled around Orkney between 1529 and 1657. He wrote down a lot of info and captured some of their native language. It wasn't Gaelic, you see, it was something called Norn, which was a corruption of the Norwegian language. Norn had died out by the nineteenth century, and we don't have many examples of it left. It was the language of the common people, you see, so very few of them could read or write. Some words remained in general use, though.' I type some more words and pull up what I want to show Billy.

But before I can do that, Billy coughs a little and looks discomfited. 'Would the word '*felkyo*' mean anything? In that language? In Norn?'

'*Felkyo*? Yes. It means witch.'

'Ahhhh.' He sucks his breath in and sits back in his seat. 'That makes a lot of sense then.'

'Was Mhairi a witch?' I grin at him.

'No. Not her . . .' His voice trails off and he looks a little more discomfited. 'At least, I don't think so.'

I smile, then move the screen towards my companion. 'See? Jo Ben's original Orkney manuscript was in Latin, and it was discovered in the Advocates Library in a book called *History of Orkney*.'

'The Advocates Library? Here? In Edinburgh? But I thought that was just law?'

'Mainly, yes. But it's maybe somewhere for you to look if we can't find what we need here. If not — ' I shrug ' — the National Library of Scotland might be able to help. They've got most of the non-law stuff from Advocates.'

'Wow.' Billy looks impressed. 'You know a lot about this, don't you?'

'I get paid to do it.' I tap away at the screen again. 'Look — this is what I'm researching for my family tree. I suspect we've got links to the Jacobites too, only for some reason, my lot come from Devon.' I show him the notes I've already made. 'My family seems to hail from Clovelly — a smugglers' paradise.'

'Ah! The smugglers.' He grins. 'I've heard pirating tales aplenty from there. Didn't a lot of Spanish pirates leave part of their genetic pool down there?'

I laugh and I try to muffle it, so it comes out more like a snort. I look around quickly, as it seems a lot louder when I laugh like that in a library for some reason. Nobody flinches, thank goodness.

'You could say that. They did leave a lot of local ladies pregnant around that coastline, I believe. This is why I think I've got smugglers' blood in me — but the thing that makes me think I've got Jacobite origins too is the fact that this was recorded in an old letter my great

127

gran had hidden in her jewellery box.'
I show him a scan of the most precious
document in my genealogy arsenal.

It's just a brief note asking after the
health of one of my eighteenth-century
relatives, a young boy called Charles
Oke. It has a drawing of a rose on it with
a bud next to it, and underneath the picture are four words:

Fiat et Revirescit.
Amen.

'It sort of means 'Let it come to pass','
I explain to Billy, 'and that they hope the
Prince will return. Then of course Amen
means 'let it be thus'. The white rose is, I
think, the Jacobite rose, and the little bud
signifies Prince Charles Edward Stuart — and it all leads to 'the King over
the water'. Especially as the oak leaf was
another Jacobite symbol — so Charles
Oke, although it was a fairly common
Clovelly surname, might have a different connotation. A double meaning.
Ta-dah!' I look at him and hope he's as
excited as I am about it. He does look a
bit blown away. 'And, the address on the

back of the letter is the Tolbooth prison.'

'Wow. You've got more to go on than I have.' He's silent for a moment. 'Much more. I don't think I'm going to get anywhere near that with poor old Mhairi.'

'You never know.' I pull the screen back towards me. 'Sometimes it just takes one stroke of luck and it sets you off in the proper direction.'

'I suppose Mhairi would stand a good chance of being Jacobite-ish, wouldn't she? In that timeframe?'

'Yes. And, if she's from Orkney, they were a Jacobite stronghold up there.' I nudge him, I hope playfully and not too familiarly. 'I wonder what she got up to with the Jacobites? Now *that* would be interesting to know.'

'That *would* be interesting.'

I smile, shake my head and go back to my search engine. 'My problem is that I just can't make the connection between little Charles Oke and Scotland. No idea why a prisoner in the Tolbooth would send a letter all the way to Devon to ask about a little boy. I'm pretty sure there should be a connection, though.'

And I know I'm preaching to Billy about just needing one stroke of luck, but I'm not about to confess that this one is the one I need the stroke of luck for — little Charles Oke and whichever Jacobites were possibly linked to him have evaded me for bloody ages. This trip to Edinburgh could be my last hope of finding anything out about him . . .

Billy

I am stunned, absolutely stunned, at the enthusiasm and knowledge this girl possesses. I mean, I love history and know quite a bit, but she's one step higher than me in the Applied Knowledge front.

I really want to help her. I actually feel as if we've got more chance of finding information out about her family than I have of finding out much about my ghostly friend.

I'm not sure what to do.

I drum my fingers on the table for a

second, then suddenly I have an idea. 'The Tolbooth.'

'Excuse me?'

'The Tolbooth records. If we can find anything out about people who were incarcerated there around about the time Charles Oke lived, you might be able to make a connection. I know he was only young, but you've got a timeframe he lived in as a starting point. Perhaps he has an older relative in there? Someone with the same surname? He was obviously linked to a prisoner in there.'

'True . . .' She processes the information. 'I have tried that, though, but I've had no luck. The resources are quite limited online, and I can't find the connection to Charles. It's a rabbit hole. I thought by coming up here I could see the physical records; maybe see something that's not accessible virtually.'

'Hmm. And I guess, thinking about it, there's possibly no reason that the prisoner would have the same name as Charles, is there? He or she may be a family friend. And perhaps a fresh set of eyes would help you?'

'Thank you. But what about your Mhairi?'

'Well perhaps you could help me find her in exchange? The Tolbooth info you need might be at the Advocates Library, so we could start there.'

'I think the Tolbooth info is with the National Records of Scotland. Possibly at General Register House, which is why I'm going to try there too. But the Advocates Library might be good because there might be legal records there. Trials and such. It's worth a look.' She raises her hand, palm outwards and holds it in front of me. I understand we need to high five on this agreement, and so I do.

There's a little zing of electricity as our palms connect and her eyes widen slightly. I'm certain mine do the same.

'Right. Okay.' She busies herself with her laptop again, but I see the faint blush that tinges her cheeks. 'Back to work. I say we do a couple of hours here, then lunch, then see what we can get at the Advocates, yes?'

'Sounds good.' I move my seat a little further away from her, fighting every instinct in my body to move closer to her and take her in my arms and . . . 'Right! I'm off to find my own computer.' I smile at her, too brightly it seems, as she looks a little taken aback when she turns to face me again. Maybe I look like a vampire. The McCreadie Winning Smile my brothers and I trained long and hard to achieve normally does that — wins people over, that is — but in extreme cases, when we try too hard, it can look freakish and scary.

I rearrange my face and clear my throat. I point to a bank of computers at a long desk against the wall. 'I'll go over there. I'll catch up with you in two hours.'

'See you then. Good luck. Oh!' She hastily scribbles some websites down in her notebook and tears the page out. 'These are useful ones to start with. Have fun.'

'Thanks.' I take the page from her and look at it.

The page is edged with mint-green, and her loopy handwriting is in sea-blue ink.

It looks like the colour scheme of a mermaid.

Lexie

The two hours pass very quickly. I must confess I'm clock-watching a little as I explore all the avenues I can think of, but I still can't find anything to link me to Charles Oke.

I've managed, over the years I've been researching my family tree, to trace my family *down* from Charles — but never back up. It's like he didn't exist before he was plopped, seagull-like, onto the pages of my family history.

All I have referencing him is the letter from Tolbooth prison. It mentions 'the babe', so Charles must have only been a small baby at the time, and the decorations on it do, as I told Billy, seem to imply that the family had Jacobite tendencies. Even if I broaden my range to several years before the 1745 rebellion, where Bonnie Prince Charlie really came to the fore, nothing comes up. I've sourced the address the letter went to — it was a tavern, so I'm assuming the family may even have been lodgers there, then decided to settle down. But every road I take is a dead end.

It is *so* frustrating.

But I do like the Tolbooth idea — the idea of spending a portion of condensed time with Billy McCreadie, poring over the records and trying to fit the pieces of the jigsaw together —

'Any luck?' His voice, coming from just over my shoulder, startles me and brings me out of my reverie.

'Not really. You?'

He holds the sheet of paper up. 'I've found out a wee bit of information about Orkney at that time. You're right — they loved the Jacobites up there. After the 1715 rebellion, a lot of Jacobites were helped on to safety in Sweden after they ran north from mainland Scotland to the islands. Then in 1745, during the second uprising — the one that me and you are both more interested in, I guess — the Jacobite lairds made sure that Orkney was a safe place to land supplies to help them. Orkney held out until a month after Culloden, so it was rife with Jacobites to the very end. And, more importantly, safe. And guess what — a lot of the supplies came from Spain.'

'Wow. A strong link to piratical Spaniards there as well. How exciting.'

Then he says something that is so outrageous that it couldn't possibly be true. 'Spanish smugglers. And Orkney. In the right timeframe.' He raises an eyebrow and, it has to be said, he looks divine. 'There could well be a link — couldn't there?'

And then I think, why *couldn't* it be true?

And I suddenly want to find out whether it is with Billy, more than anything else in the world.

Except I need some lunch first.

I'm suddenly really hungry, and I never could work on an empty tummy.

7

Billy

It's a very strange idea that the two people we are looking for might have known each other — or, at least, Mhairi might have known a bit about some of the smugglers potentially related to Lexie.

'Imagine. Mhairi might have seen your old Spanish ancestor. It's like that poem: 'If you wake at midnight, and hear a horse's feet, Don't go drawing back the blind, or looking in the street, Them that ask no questions isn't told a lie. Watch the wall my darling while the Gentlemen go by'.' I grin as I recite the words of Kipling's 'A Smuggler's Song'.

'I love it.' Lexie smiles up at me as she closes her laptop and zips it up into its case. 'It's romantic in a way. A dark-haired piratical type and all that . . . ' A flush creeps across her cheeks again, and she shoves the laptop case roughly into her huge bag.

137

'Mmm. And perhaps how that dark-haired piratical type met a beautiful stranger in the most random of circumstances. With a big fat black cat in tow.' The flush deepens, but I see a twitch of her lips as she fights against a smile. She knows, I hope, that I mean her.

'Sure. Right. Lunch. Yeah?' She stands up and hitches the bag on her shoulder. 'I didn't get anything as interesting as you. Just a zillion more dead ends.' She sighs and shakes her head. 'I'm holding out for a miracle in the records place.' She raises her hand and crosses her fingers at me. It's a bit reminiscent of Mhairi's witch-sign.

We walk out of the library and meander to the nearest sandwich shop to grab lunch.

We've just settled onto a bench in Princes Street Gardens where we can have our picnic when my mobile rings.

'Hello, Nessa.'

'Hello, William. My favourite piratical brother!'

I roll my eyes and shake my head at

Lexie, who's opening a bag of crisps. 'Nessa,' I mouth, and she grins.

'Aye, aye. What do you want?'

'Aye, aye? Should it not be *Arrr, arrrr*?' Nessa giggles and I stare at the phone.

'Are you drunk, Agnes?'

"*Arrr, arrrr,* you drunk.' Hee hee hee . . . ' She sniggers, and, yes, it seems she is indeed drunk. 'We're out celebrating our engagement. We're having a champagne lunch at The Witchery.' She names her favourite restaurant in Edinburgh, right at the foot of the castle. It just always had to be her favourite with that name.

'Lovely,' I say flatly. I love my sister, but she's annoying as hell when she's drunk.

'The reason I'm phoning is to ask you a question.'

'No. I'm not babysitting Schubert. It's Alfie's turn.'

'No, no, no.' There's a rustle and I think she must be shaking her head. 'Schubert is fine. He's *fine*. He's off on a little walk.'

So that means, somewhere in Edinburgh, is a massive black cat holding a purple lead in his mouth.

'Okay,' I say. 'So, what do you want me for?'

'I just want to ask you a question. Billy — ' She takes a deep breath. 'Have you found what you're looking for? Or have you *still* haven't found what you're looking for . . . ?' She collapses into a honky sort of laughter, and I close my eyes in despair.

Even more U2 references. Funny, funny girl.

Not.

There's another crackly noise and Ewan takes over the call. 'Sorry, Billy. She's had way too much to drink. I'm taking her home soon.'

'The grammar didn't even make sense,' I grumble.

'I know. I know. Nessa — what? What is it?'

'Tell him to look in the library — the other library.' Her voice comes back onto the call faintly. 'The *other* library.

140

And the records. The *records*.'

Then there's the sound of a crash, and Nessa going 'Whoopsadaisy' and Ewan going, 'Sorry, sorry, mate. She's knocked the bottle over — sorry. Sorry.'

I shake my head. 'Have fun.' Then I hang up.

Moments later, a text comes in.

ttTrRy theeee othRa librrarrry adn rceooords.lo Veeyuo!!!!!!!!!!! I haVnigfuuuuu-unnnnnnn!!!! xxxxxxxxxxxxxxxxxxxxxxxx

Even her texts are drunk. I ignore it and turn my attention back to Lexie. 'My sister. She's out celebrating. She needs to go home. But she's saying we should try the other library.'

'The other library? What does she mean? And how does she even *know*?' Lexie looks, quite rightly, stunned, and pauses with a crisp halfway to her mouth.

'My sister just does,' I say darkly. Then, before I can stop myself, I hear myself add: 'You'll find out. You'll get used to it.'

141

I almost choke on my crisp. That sounds like he's intending to have me in his future.

It's not a disagreeable thought.

I answer very carefully. 'Cool. Great. I look forward to it.'

He visibly relaxes and takes a swig of cola like it's piratical rum. 'Cool.' He stares off into the distance and I stare as well; it's sort of a companionable staring, where neither of us seems to feel that we have to say anything to fill in the gaps.

All too soon lunch is over, and we gather together the wrappers and the empty bottles and dispose of them.

'Okay. The Advocates Library. This way.' Billy points. 'Towards Parliament Square. The National Library of Scotland is attached to it, so we get two for the price of one.'

'And where's the records place?'

'Not very far from it, along by the train station.'

'Maybe we should do the records first?

Find the Tolbooth information, then translate that into the legal side of thing?'

'Good idea. We should have time to do both if — oh!' He stops and looks at me. 'I never thought. What if you've got to book in?'

I grin. 'I'm an archivist. Let me use a little bit of influence . . .'

And so I do.

We soon find ourselves in the records office, standing in the midst of shelves and shelves of books and papers, and it's all quite overwhelming. Wonderful, but overwhelming. Even for me.

'The Tolbooth.' I look around, and I'm sure there must be criminal records in here I can actually get my hands on. I'm quite excited by the prospect. In fact—

'Mow wow.'

We look at each other.

'Did you hear . . . ?'

'Was that . . . ?'

'*Schubert*?' we chorus together. We both turn around, searching for him. His voice was echoey and somewhat muffled, which leads me to believe that he's well hidden somewhere — because how, otherwise, could a fat black cat shimmy his way in here during his constitutional and not be located?

'Mow wow!' Schubert's voice is more urgent, and there's a definite hint of rustle to it. Then a scrabble and a clunk; the sound of something falling from a shelf and another indignant 'mow wow', followed by a muttering, grumpy growl.

'He's in amongst the records. The little bugger!' Billy strides off in the general direction of his sister's cat.

I watch him go, my jaw slack and hanging down in astonishment. What on God's green earth is Schubert doing in here?

But I soon find out.

Billy appears from behind a shelving unit, clutching a purple lead in one hand and an old, leather-bound book in the other. Schubert is, of course, attached to the lead, and he's walking prettily along until he sees me, then he starts pulling and pulling and, eventually, I hurry over to them and usher them back into the dark depths at the end of the shelving unit.

'Mow wow,' Schubert says ever so politely and, almost automatically, I bend down and pat him.

'Yes. Your guess is as good as mine!' Billy looks furious. 'I doubt Nessa knew he'd got himself stuck in here — oh. Wait. Ha!' He laughs shortly. 'Who am I kidding? Those two know each other ridiculously well. He's like her familiar or something — ' He bites his lip as if he's said too much.

'A familiar. Good. Okay.' I give Schubert a final rub between his ears, and he purrs like a chainsaw. 'He's in the records office. And she mentioned trying the other library and the records office for our purposes.' I shrug. 'Shall we just leave it at that?'

'Yes.'

'What did he find?'

'Excuse me?' The question seems to throw him.

'What did he find? You've got something in your hand. He must have been having a good look around.' I smile to show I'm joking.

'It's a ledger of some kind.' He opens the book, and Schubert sits down nicely and starts making a tuneful mewing sound as if he's singing a nonchalant song. He's a very characterful cat, I must say, as well as having lots of personality and being generally quite funky.

'He knocked it off the shelf he was sitting on. Do you know —' Billy still looks mad ' — that he was right at the top of one of those shelves? Over there.' He gesticulates furiously.

I look at the book he has in his hand; it appears very dusty, as if it's been sitting on a shelf for a very long time. 'It does look old,' I comment.

Billy carefully opens the book. He scans the pages quickly, then his eyes flick over them again, more slowly. The edges of the sheets are ripped and brown with age. Billy will have to be careful, as sometimes the stitching comes away from the spine and the page falls out — I don't think we'll be popular if we destroy records in the records office.

Schubert yawns and settles down.

'Does anyone hear a cat in here?' pipes up an old lady who's sitting sifting through a microfilm. 'I'm sure I heard a cat.'

I quickly drop my laptop bag on the floor, sort of making a barricade so Schubert can't be spotted behind it, then drop my coat on top of that again. Schubert makes himself very small — well, very small for him — and, unless anybody was wondering what Billy had attached to the end of the purple lead, he's as well hidden as he can be.

We ignore the woman and huddle closer, trying to establish what's written on the pages Billy holds.

'It's old prison records. From the Tolbooth, I think.' He checks the spine. There are a series of dates written on the spine in gold-blocking, covering some months from 1745–1746, and I can see what looks like rows and rows of names inside the book. Billy pushes the centre of the book together, smoothing the creases out of the paper and flips carefully through the pages.

The poor old book looks as if it's going to drop to bits any moment now. The archivist in me wants to wrap it up in cotton wool. The excited genealogist wants to tear it out of his hands and rifle through the pages, hunting out names that look anything like 'Oke'.

Then Billy pauses and shrugs, somewhere in the midst of 1745, casting a quizzical glance up at me. 'It's within our date range. It's prison records. It may be as good a place to start as any. Unless you have a strategy?'

'It *is* within our date range. One of many ledgers, I bet, though.' I peer more closely at the spidery ink and notice there are notes beside a few of the names, and some are quite lengthy. Some are just one or two words. There's also a column at the end of each entry which seems to record the sentences dealt out. Theft, robbery, pickpocketing, assault, drunk and disorderly behaviour — everything that one might find in a police record book or a prison ledger is in there, with one particularly exciting entry that I can't stop staring at.

If I did have a strategy, it's gone out of the window. 'Ooh.' There's a very Irish-sounding chap called Lewis Martin S O'Shea. *What a mouthful*. His crime, it is noted, is 'piracy'. 'Wow. So, there were pirates around here,' I whisper, staring at the man's name. I look up at Billy. '*This* is what I mean by a rabbit hole. A veritable rabbit hole.'

'It's a great rabbit hole.' He points at the name. 'This chap would be cool to research, wouldn't he? But he's Irish, so he's probably nothing to do with either of us.'

'Exactly. But look what happened to him.' It's my turn to point to the entry as I unravel the ancient copperplate scrawl. 'Tried at Admiralty Court. Found guilty of piracy. Taken to Leith and executed twixt the high and low water marks. They did that 'twixt' thing to pirates to make a point.'

'And we can see that it happened in 1745. Exactly when we need it.' Billy smiles wryly. 'Oh, why can't our people have any connection to Lewis Martin S O'Shea?'

'*What?*' My heart jumps and I stare at Billy. 'Say it again. Say his name again.'

'Lewis Martin S O'Shea.' He smiles a lopsided smile at me. 'It's cool. It's a cool name. Hardly trips off the tongue, though.'

'But Martin S . . . Martin*ez*. It could be Spanish, couldn't it?'

'Martinez. It could be.' He grins again. 'But O'Shea isn't. And I don't think Lewis is.'

'No. It isn't. But what if he was saying his name in a Spanish accent? And Lewis could be Spanish, if it was spelt L-U-I-S. If it was an unfamiliar name, they'd just write it down as they heard it. They wouldn't care what it really was. They'd just want to do justice. Okay. Okay . . . ' I start to get really, really excited and shake my hands around as if I'm releasing energy. Then I hold them out, straight in front of me, and stop shaking them. 'Let's look at this illogically. Logic hasn't helped either of us. And God knows I've invested more hours than I can count looking into my family history — '

'Mow wow.' There's a muffled Schubert noise from behind the barricade. 'Mow wow.'

Billy closes the book and looks down at the cat. 'Nessa said to try the records place and the other library. And I guess we found Schubert here . . . '

' . . . sitting on a shelf with a ledger on it . . . '

' . . . with a pirate's name in it . . . '

' . . . from a Jacobite timeframe . . . ' I start to giggle. 'No. No. It's bonkers, isn't it? Crazy.'

'It is.' Billy nods. 'But this is my family we're talking about. Nessa and Schubert. I'm inclined to give it a go.'

Billy

I say those words and I can't believe I've actually said them out loud. 'Give it a go'. Give *what* a go? A random

151

coincidence facilitated by a damn black cat based on a throwaway comment from a drunk woman?

'Luis Martinez O'Shea,' I murmur. 'Okay. Well, I think we need to head to the Advocates Library. Try to find out about this guy's trial. It's practically over the road. It's not a very *deep* rabbit hole, is it?'

I cannot believe I'm saying it. I cannot believe I'm *doing* it.

'Not yet,' says Lexie. 'But trust me. We could fall for a very long time into it. He could be Mhairi's Jacobite smuggler friend from the Orkneys, or my potential Jacobite relation. What are we going to do with Schubert?'

'Will he fit into your laptop bag?' I'm only half-joking. I have no idea what we're going to do with Schubert. I don't want to eat into our time by taking him home.

'Not really. Is there anyone around who can pick him up and take him home?'

'Ah.' I grin. 'We're not far from Maria's

café. I'll take him there. Maria will have him for a bit. And if Hugo is there, even bloody better. He can have him.'

'Okay. Tell you what. Shall I head into the Advocates Library and start looking for our pirate's trial? Then you can meet me there.'

'Sounds like a plan.' I catch her eye for a moment, and then it all happens quite quickly. We lean into one another and I kiss her, very gently, on the lips. 'See you soon.'

'See you soon.' There's a smile turning the edges of her lips up-a-ways, and now I know what it's like to kiss a girl with a silver lip-ring.

It's nice.

It's very nice indeed.

★ ★ ★

I hurry as fast as I can, dragging a fat, grumbling black cat on a purple lead to Thistledean Café. And, joy of joys, Hugo is in there making a fancy coffee for a customer.

I hang back and bide my time, but as we walk in I can see Hugo's suave smile slip and waiver as he catches sight of us out of the corner of his eye.

'Good afternoon,' I say eventually.

'No,' says Hugo.

'I beg your pardon?'

'No. I'm not taking the Beast.'

'I think you are. You, matey boy — ' I point my finger at him. ' — have to take your turn. You've got Isla. This is my chance to get someone nice.'

'What about Vanessa? She was nice.' He eyes the Beast in disgust. I know he's simply playing for time.

'You're simply playing for time,' I tell him. 'Vanessa was not nice. Vanessa was the exact *opposite* of nice. But Lexie . . . Lexie is *very* nice.'

'Mow wow.' Schubert glares at my brother, and I feel, I do honestly feel, that he's actually backing me up.

'See? Schubert agrees with me. I need to get back to the library — '

'To borrow a U2 album, circa 1987?'

'To meet Lexie and look up Luis

Martinez O'Shea.'

'What the *hell*?'

'He's a pirate.' I feel affronted on Luis Martinez O'Shea's account. 'We're researching him.'

Hugo looks at me and laughs and laughs. 'I cannot believe you're spending the day in a library researching a bloke with a funny name.'

'Well I am. So please — look after Schubert for me. Nessa is pissed and incapable.'

'Oh God.' Hugo closes his eyes and holds out his hand for the lead. 'You owe me. Big time.'

'Oh! Hey, Schubert! Hey, Billy!' Maria materialises out of the back and squats down, fussing over the Beast, who obligingly falls onto his side then struggles onto his back so she can rub his tummy while he waves his ridiculously fat little legs in the air in ecstasy. 'I caught some of that. Who's this pirate dude you're after?'

'Luis Martinez O'Shea.' I pull a face. 'He's maybe Irish, maybe Spanish, quite possibly interesting. I don't know. The

155

guy who wrote it down two hundred years ago didn't seem to know either.' I shrug my shoulders.

'O'Shea? Is it not Ochoa?' Maria looks confused. 'If he's Spanish, that is. Sounds a bit similar if you're not used to the language.'

'Ochoa? What do you mean?'

Maria is Italian, although she's lived in Edinburgh most of her life. 'Just saying, if he's already got Martinez in his name, the rest of it may well be Ochoa. I suspect a Scottish judge from two hundred years ago was just interested in getting him through the system and out the other side, and obviously wouldn't have been bothered with spelling his name correctly. I met a Pedro Ochoa once, when I was a student. I went to Barcelona for the summer. He was *hot*.' She kisses her fingertips and grins wickedly. 'Then I came home and met Stu.' She sighs and goes back to rubbing Schubert's belly. 'I met Stu.'

'How do you spell Ochoa?' I ask tentatively.

'O-c-h-o-a.'

My mind starts working overtime. It's not a million miles away from Oke, is it? *Is* it? If you were trying to hide your identity or suchlike . . .

My heart thumps against my chest, and I look at Schubert.

'Mow wow,' he mumbles, then looks at me slyly before he goes back to writhing in pleasure over Maria's ministrations.

'I have to go.' I turn around and run out of that café as fast as I can. I need to get to that library and back to Lexie as soon as humanly possible.

8

Lexie

I'm turning over the pages of the most fascinating document I've ever set eyes on, and there's still loads to read.

But what a treasure.

And what a bloody brilliant rabbit hole.

I have, in my hands, the transcript of Lewis Martin S O'Shea's trial. He's definitely a Lewis here, not a Luis — but a judge who wanted to hang a pirate wouldn't really care about the detail, would they?

It all started, as we discovered, in the spring of 1745. O'Shea was a pirate, so they say, and his ship was wrecked off the coast of Argyll with the loss of several lives.

The captain was a French-born chap, Pierre du Casse, and several of the crew were rounded up and taken to Edinburgh Castle. A handful evaded capture, so the trial documentation says, and apparently they went on the run. A couple died in prison, another two escaped, and by the end of it all, our friend here was the only one remaining to be tried for piracy. The judge decided he was guilty on the basis that the jury consisted of ship owners and merchants and, as we'd already discovered, he was dragged to the seaside at Leith and hung 'twixt the high and low water marks' as they so poetically put it:

The Pirate is to be taken to the Sands of Leith within the Flood-mark, upon Wednesday next, betwixt the Hours of Eleven a Clock in the Forenoon, and Four a Clock in the Afternoon, and there to be Hanged upon a Gibbet till he be Dead.

Ugh.

Awful.

And I doubt, I very much sincerely doubt, that this guy was Irish . . .

'I don't think he was Irish. I think he was Spanish!' I jump as Billy appears, seemingly out of nowhere, his voice urgent. He's looking rather deliciously dishevelled, as if he's been running across the town. 'I ran all the way here,' he continues, 'all the way across town to tell you. I don't think he was Irish.'

'I'm reading his trial,' I offer, pointing ineffectually at the paperwork. 'He was on a French ship that got wrecked. There were some survivors and some casualties, and he's the only one who got hung —'

'I think he wasn't called O'Shea.' Billy's eyes are a little wild and looking into them does funny things to the pit of my stomach. 'Sorry — sorry. I shouldn't interrupt.'

'No, you should. You *should* interrupt. If you've got information about Lewis Martin S O'Shea, that is.'

'It's a hunch, more than information — but Maria from the café thinks his surname might have been Ochoa. She says it's Spanish, and I think it makes sense. Doesn't it?' He looks hopeful as if I need to validate his theories.

'Well, yes. It does. Luis Martinez Ochoa.' A little shiver runs down my spine. He sounds rather splendid.

'And Ochoa — it's not a million miles away from Oke. Is it?'

'Oh! I never thought of that. It's not really *that* similar, though, is it?'

'It is similar enough if you need to hide your identity. If you had, say, a descendant who was taken down the west coast of Scotland and Wales and then England, and then ended up in Devon . . .'

He pauses, and it's as if something goes *ker-clunk* inside me. 'Oh . . .'

'Yes. Oh.' We stare at each other for a moment.

'I haven't finished reading this yet,' I say in a silly, small voice. 'It might, if I keep reading, tell us more about where he allegedly came from.'

'I won't disturb you, then. I'll sit here. And think. And you can tell me what it says.'

'Okay.' I lower my eyes and read, very quickly, more about our new friend Luis.

Then I read it again.

And again.

Then I feel ever so slightly sick from a sort of suppressed excitement.

'They came via Orkney,' I say, eventually. 'Around the top of Scotland. Up from Spain. Via France. Via Orkney. Around the top. And down again. Then they wrecked at Argyll.'

'Seriously?'

I swallow. 'They found an Amen glass on his person. And a note in French listing some names that were known members of the Stuart court in France, along with some French coins and a small, silver bracelet engraved with the Stuart rose . . . and the words *Fiat et Revirescit*. The same words that are in the letter to Charles Oke's guardians.'

'An Amen glass?' Billy frowns. 'Didn't they get smashed after they drank toasts to the Stuart King? The King over the water?'

'Yes. There are only about thirty-seven around now. They were massively treasonable. Engraved with all sorts of Jacobite propaganda. Absolutely beautiful, though.'

'Pretty compelling evidence against Luis then. They knew where his loyalties lay.'

'Damning evidence, I would say.' I look at the page in front of me, and I'm ashamed to notice the words are blurring as my eyes fill up with silly tears for this guy who I'd never even heard about before today. 'He was caught at the absolute worst time. Perhaps he was helping to prepare for Culloden?'

The Battle of Culloden, the final push for the Jacobites where they tried in vain to fight for their King and reinstate him, was in 1746, but the uprising had started in 1745.

'At least he wasn't carved into pieces at Culloden by the Redcoats with all the other Highlanders,' says Billy. He looks at me and half-smiles. 'Yeah. It's not great, whatever way you look at it.'

'Nope.' I wipe away the tears and try to smile. 'Ah well. He's nothing to me, is he? Don't know why I'm getting flustered.'

'Because you're a nice person.' Billy leans across and takes my hand in his. His hand is warm, and it makes me feel safe. 'Are we in agreement that Schubert might have indirectly directed us to Luis Martinez Ochoa and his Jacobite leanings? And his Orkney visits?'

I laugh, a little bit weepily, but it is a laugh. 'I agree. Bonkers.'

'Bonkers. Good. Lexie — if I suggest something to you that sounds equally bonkers, will you promise not to run screaming away from me or to think I'm irredeemably bonkers?'

'I can't run away,' I say in surprise. 'You've got hold of my hand.'

'Good.' He squeezes my hand a little tighter and it makes me smile. 'I think it's time you met Mhairi.'

Billy

'Mhairi?' Lexie stares at me, the smile slipping off her face. I hold onto her hand, making sure she can't run away shrieking until she hears me out.

'Yes. Mhairi. Will you come to Greyfriars with me again? Now? Please?'

'Oh!' Her face clears and she laughs. She squeezes my hand in return. 'She's buried there! Of course. I love looking at old tombstones. Just let me write up these notes, then I'll happily come with you.'

'Cool.' I leave go of her hand and sit back in the seat. My heart is pounding like crazy, and I'm almost surprised that she can't hear it.

Part of me is still worried that once she finds out it's not exactly a gravestone we're going to look at, she'll run off screaming.

But I have to try it. I have to give it a go. I would guess that, even if there is no connection at all between Mhairi and Luis, that she would have at least heard tales about the ships docking there with supplies. But if there was anything else . . . anything else that might bind me and Lexie together . . .

Both Mhairi and Nessa's voices come back and, literally, haunt me.

A binding spell.

My heart turns one more somersault.

I truly think I would have fallen for — *had* already fallen for — Lexie Farrington, long before young Isabel McCreadie decided to meddle.

That's a point — should I perhaps tell Scott about his daughter's dubious talents in witchcraft? Or is Nessa the best one to approach him about it? A conundrum indeed. But not one I'm going to think about today.

'Done.' Lexie closes her notebook and then, reluctantly, closes the book containing the trial records. 'I know where to find them if I need to come back. Somehow, I don't want to look anyone else up today. Do you know what I mean? I'm too full of Luis to think about anyone else at the minute. I think I'd like to finish his story, then go back to my Charles.'

'Maybe it's all the same story? Maybe Luis and Charles are linked? Maybe even Mhairi is linked to them?' I grin and shrug. 'Maybe Luis and Mhairi were hellbound together. Both wild and exciting — an Orkney lass wanting more than the Islands and a dashing Spaniard wanting — well — an Orkney lass.'

'Bonkers! Is Schubert all right? I didn't ask.'

'He's fine. Come on.' I pick her laptop bag up and sling it over my shoulder, then hold my hand out for her to take, should she want to.

She takes it.

We leave the Advocates Library together and walk to Greyfriars Kirkyard, also together.

Lexie

We stroll to the kirkyard hand in hand, and it all feels very different to when I came to the tour Billy was running. It feels as if we have all the time in the world — everything *looks* different too.

Of course, it's probably just because it's daylight now, and I know Billy better. It feels as if it's the right thing to do, to be walking down these old streets holding his hand. Like the streets and the town are woven into my soul, somehow.

I feel a lot more at home here in Edinburgh than I thought I might. It's nice. It's a welcoming city, and I've met some incredible people. It's a shame I have to go home quite soon, but I intend to make the most of the time I still have here.

I already feel a little sad about leaving, if I'm honest.

I think about it, and think *really* hard, about where I could travel to next. Where else could I drive to and explore next time I have some time off work? Or next time I decide to change career? Or next time I decide to move on? The Dales still *sound* quite nice, but . . .

No. There's nowhere, really. Nowhere that's calling to me: which is quite odd. I rarely ever go back to any of the places I've been to. I've got a book called *100 Mystical Sites* in the UK, and my intention is to visit each and every one of them. Or at least it was my intention. I'm not so sure now.

I think I like Edinburgh too much. I really don't want to leave.

Still, I can always come back.

Come back.

The words thrill me and send a shiver of something up my spine. I dip my head and smile to myself, because it all sounds a little bonkers and melodramatic, doesn't it?

All too soon, we reach the gates of Greyfriars Kirkyard and I notice Billy hanging back a little.

He looks around the place and holds onto the bars of the gate with his spare hand. It's like he's searching for something or someone. It's a different set of gates to the ones we used for the tour. There are a set of steps behind these ones, and they look rather eerie and Gothic.

Billy is looking up at the top of them. He freezes, then swears under his breath, then throws the gate open. He leads me purposefully up the steps, still holding my hand, and I follow, trying to see what he's got his eye on; he's facing straight forwards and his jaw is set. There's that tiny muscle twitching in his cheek, and I feel my tummy start to churn and my heart begin to thump.

There's a strange feeling to the steps, as they curve ever so slightly to the left and we climb up them; almost as if they are a gathering place, harbouring spirits or souls or whatever you want to call them.

And I don't believe in ghosts, so that is saying something, coming from me.

'Here,' Billy says, continuing until we reach the mortsafe we'd had our tea at during the tour. 'Just here.' He looks around, frowning, and murmurs very quietly, 'come on. I saw you. I *saw* you, Mhairi Clouston. Come *on*.'

Then it all seems to happen at once.

His hand tightens in mine, and I suddenly feel as if I've been punched in the stomach. All the air has gone out of my lungs, and there's a freezing wind that whips up out of nowhere in the deserted kirkyard.

I open my mouth to scream, then think better of it, reminding myself sharply that I am practical and not easily scared. Yet I still turn instinctively into Billy's shoulder, hiding my face. He pulls me close, and there's an overwhelming smell of saltwater and seaweed and ocean breezes. There's a rushing in my ears and then I hear a voice, which is impossible — hadn't we just been alone five seconds ago?

'You! Ye came back then? Aye. Aboot time, aboot *time* too! I'm still here, as ye can see, aye, still here . . . I'm not going naewhere, am I? *Am* I?"

'Mhairi. How pleasant to see you again. Even though it's only a matter of a few short hours since we last spoke.' Billy's voice is flat and it brings me up short. It's not the sort of voice I'd have expected him to use when he was greeting anyone — but *Mhairi*? I thought she was dead? I thought she was some Jacobite relation that he—

Curiosity gets the better of me and I open my eyes against his shirt. I slowly turn away from the warm safety of his chest to see what this woman looks like, this woman with the bonkers accent that's not quite Scottish, not quite Gaelic and not quite, I think, Norwegian.

And when I see her, the world beyond her goes all woozy. My jaw drops open and I can't stop staring at her.

She's standing there, her hands on her hips, her face furious, her hair wild and blonde and tangled. It's blowing about in a wind that only seems to be near us, judging by the still tufts of grass and tree branches I see out of the corner of my vision.

She seems solid enough but here and there, around her edges, I can see straight through, as if I'm looking into a mist and the world is grey and eerie beyond it. Faint shapes of tombstones and mausoleums shift and change and blur beyond her and, as I stare, a puddle forms around her feet, and water drips off her elbows and off the hem of her dress.

'D'ye see me? *Do* ye?'

For a moment I'm not sure who she's talking to, but then I realise it's me. My gaze travels from the top of her matted curls to the dripping hem of her tartan skirt dragging along the ground as she begins to pace to and fro, her eyes never leaving mine. 'D'ye *see* me? Ye didn't yon last time, did ye? No, no, you didnae ... well ye *might* ha' done . . .'

'Lexie.' Billy sounds defeated. 'She's asking . . . never mind. This was a stupid idea. A really stupid idea.'

I can't even bring myself to speak, but I feel my mouth is opening and closing on its own anyway. This woman, or whatever she is, has fixed her eyes on mine, and there's something that I recognise in them — some sort of connection that I can't quite explain — that's making me deny the apparent stupidity of the idea. Then I tear my gaze away and shake my head. *I don't believe in ghosts.* 'Actually. Yes. Yes, it *is* stupid, because I don't believe in ghosts.' It seems I'm trying to convince myself more than anyone else around — living or dead. A chill creeps up my spine and around my shoulders, and I shudder. 'I don't. I *don't*. They're not *real*.'

I start to hyperventilate, and the world

goes a bit more woozy.

Maybe I'm *not* so practical, and maybe I *do* scare a little more easily in the presence of an apparently real ghost . . .

I drop Billy's hand and sit down suddenly on the grass, with a *flumph* to rival Schubert's. 'A ghost. She's a ghost. She wasn't your ex-girlfriend. I saw her . . . her . . . *skirt* on the tour . . . '

'Ghosts are real, Lexie,' says Billy softly. 'I see them all the time.' He sits down next to me but doesn't touch me, which is possibly just as well.

Then I start shaking. 'But they — they . . . And what the — what the — ' I do honestly think I'm going to die myself, right there and then. I've lost the ability to string a sentence together. A *ghost*! A bloody *ghost*! 'They can't exist. It's not logical. So many people have lived and died. They can't all be still hanging around. There's no room on the planet for them — no room. Oh God . . . could they be all over here? All over, everywhere, watching us?' I feel sick — all the cemeteries I've visited, all

174

my life. Maybe I was being watched the whole time . . .

I think I'm going to have to change my inscription:

Here lies Lexie Farrington, and her ghost quite possibly does exist, roaming around the place because she never settled in life and, ha ha, guess what? She can't even settle when she's dead.

'Like you said.' Billy's voice interrupts my thoughts. 'Logic sometimes gets us nowhere.' He sounds resigned, and he pulls his knees up and puts his arms around them. 'My world is sometimes illogical Lexie. All of us — my whole family . . . ' His voice trails off.

'Ah lassie,' the ghost — Mhairi — says. 'We all have to change what we believe in sooner or later. We're normally only here if we can't rest. Or if we have unfinished business.'

A chill ripples through me and I flinch. *Woah* — I cannot even bring myself to believe a dead person is talking to me.

But more than that — my business is *always* unfinished. I absolutely don't want to still be hanging around when I'm dead and buried!

My mouth works, even as no words formulate in my head to verbalise. I try, very hard, to speak, and eventually a squeaky sort of response comes out. 'But you *can't* exist. They *don't* exist.' Sadly, I think I'm only fooling myself right now.

'I can and I do exist.' She sounds almost proud, practically preening as she watches my discomfort — she's very smirky; yes, *smirky* is the word.

Now *that* makes me bristle.

I don't do smirky. From alive people *or* dead people.

I take a few deep breaths and pull myself together. 'Did . . . did you believe in the — ' I clear my throat ' — the Jacobites?'

The girl smiles suddenly and leans forward. 'Aye. I did. And I'm *pleased* ye *can* see me. Aye. *Pleased.*' She flaps her hand in front of my face, and I flinch. I don't know what I expected; the stench of rot and decay, quite possibly. But what I get is a stronger waft of the ocean.

'Mhairi, meet Lexie. Lexie, meet Mhairi.' Billy looks a bit sick but stands up and holds his hand out to me. I take it, and he helps me up. I don't leave go of his hand, even though I'm not quite sure what I'm thinking — part of me wants to run away with my fingers in my ears going *la la la*, and the other part, the greater part, wants to stay here with my hand in Billy's, because he's grounding me. He's actually grounding me, despite the implication that he sees this sort of stuff all the time. I puff a few more panicky breaths in and out and stare at the spectre of Mhairi.

She leans closer still and peers at me. 'Ye have his eyes. Well, I never.' Then she reaches even closer and her fingertip brushes my cheek. Part of me wants to freeze and scream, and another part is just sort of . . . accepting of it.

A ghost has touched my face. A ghost has *touched my face*.

Then, finally, at that point, I do begin to flip out a bit. 'Billy . . .' I swallow down a rising feeling of fear and sickness.

'She touched me! She touched my face!'

I glance up at him and he closes his eyes in despair. 'I know. *I know*. I saw it. I *saw* her touch your face.'

'But she has his eyes!' Mhairi swishes around to face Billy, then waggles her finger in my direction. 'His *eyes*! How did ye find her? *How*? Or is it just . . . chance? He's not . . . he's never . . . he's . . . ' she stutters in a heaving breath, then flops down so that she's sitting in a heap, her head in her arms, her knees pulled up to her face, just like Billy was before. Her shoulders begin to shake and there's a whole heap of heaving sobs and heaving bosoms going on, because that stomacher/corsety thing she's wearing pulls everything in and pops everything up, leaving little to the imagination up top.

'Good God.' Billy kind of reaches out and aims for her shoulders. It sort of seems like he's trying to pat her but his hand goes straight through, and that makes me feel sick again.

'It wasnae fair. It wasnae *fair*. Why did he have to be the ane that . . . ?' Mhairi gulps in a massive sob again, then seems to compose herself. She lifts her head and juts her chin out. 'Why him? Why not me? He should have . . . he should have. He should have saved *himself.*'

Then, it's as if a sudden bolt of lightning strikes me. I feel light-headed and faint and hang onto Billy even tighter.

'Mhairi — is it . . . is it . . . ' I swallow, thinking how crazy this is going to sound. 'Do you know Luis Martinez Ochoa?'

Oh God. I just asked a ghost a question.

Maybe soon I'll wake up and find out that this has all been a dream or a nightmare or —

Mhairi jerks her head around, and her eyes suddenly harden and glare at me. I cringe. *Okay, I thought it might be a bit far-fetched.* This isn't a story. This isn't a dream. This is real life. 'Sorry,' I mutter as she continues to stare at me. 'Yeah. Stupid. Ignore me.'

'Who the *hell* ever called him all that long name except for his mama? No! He was Luis. Just Luis. He was ma *Luis.*' Mhairi burrows her chin into her folded

179

arms again and stares out at the tomb-stones. 'And I'm stuck here, thankin' you, ya wee *felkyo*, wherever ye are, and he's — well, he's bound for bloody Hell I guess. He's more than likely in Hell. Aye. In Hell. That's where he'll be. With yon demons that ruled his arrogant, stu-pid, *eejit* soul — '

'Mhairi!' Billy cuts in and hunkers down in front of her. I wriggle my hand out of his as I'm now leaning at a weird angle, because he's down there and I'm still standing upright.

I feel conspicuous though, so I sit down again as well. *This is bloody surreal, it really is.*

'Mhairi. We found him, we know what happened to him.'

'Aye. They thought he was a pirate. They hanged him. What d'ye think I was trying to dae? I wanted to go to him, I did.' She shuffles up so she's sort of kneeling, and she presses her hands into the turf, curling angry fingers around blades of grass; I can't quite understand how she's doing that, seeing as she's a disembodied soul or whatever you want to call her.

Is this a bad time to remind myself, yet again, that I don't believe in ghosts?

Maybe.

Perhaps 'disembodied souls' are better to believe in?

I don't know.

I shake my head to get rid of those thoughts and try hard to concentrate on Mhairi and Billy again.

'Did the ship wreck over on the west?' Billy is asking. 'And did they bring him over here?'

'Aye.' Mhairi raises a pale, see-through hand and inelegantly wipes shimmery, ethereal snot from her nose. Despite what I believe, or *used* to believe anyway, watching her is fascinating. 'They caught a few of us,' she continues. 'He was carrying my things, though. He widnae let me carry them. Said it was too dangerous, and — ' she sniffles again ' — and that's what they found on him. Me and him and Ferdinand were taken away.' She shakes her head. 'And they kept us apart. And then when we got there, I dinna ken what happened really.' She looks into the distance, frowning at something only she can see. 'It wis a lang time ago, y'see. Many, many years ago.' She pauses and looks at the grass, then looks at a mortsafe and smiles ever so slightly. 'I know that there was something happened, and before I knew it, me and Ferdy, we were out of the gaol, we were away. *Away.*' She flaps her hand into the distance. 'And he did it. Luis did it so I'd be free and I'd get away. He sacrificed himself, he did. For me. For me and wee Charlie. For our wee bairn, Charlie.' Her face crumples again, and she sobs uncontrollably for a little while. 'So, then I tried to find a boat to get passage somewhere. Maybe the Islands. Maybe France.' She shrugs. 'Anywhere really. And the boat I got, the crew didn't like where my heart lay. And they found out whit ma wishes and ma beliefs were. And after they'd did what they wanted with me, which I haven't truly recalled, thank God and Odin, I ended up in the sea. And then I ended up here. In the kirkyard. No name. No nothing. Just in the ground with a wooden cross. Dear God and Odin. Whit an end tae it al'. Whit an end.'

It's horrifying; inhumane and horrifying, and I'm so pleased for her that she can't remember too much of it. I wish, I really do wish, ghost or not — okay, maybe I'm starting to believe in them, now the shock is wearing off — that I could put my arms around her and hug her, but I fear I'd fall right through her. I settle for edging closer to Billy, and I feel his hand creep across the grass and cover mine again.

'It wis his christening bracelet Luis had on him as well. Wee Charlie's. It wis all engraved with yon fancy words, the words we all learned by heart. *Fiat et Revirescit*. I ken we'd planned that if the worst should happen, and it did — the very worst happened — that Charlie wid be cared for by our friends in Devon, and he'd change his name so he could hide away.' She looks at me at that point.

'Did that happen? Did ma bairn get to Devon?'

I swallow. 'Yes. Yes, he did. We found out about the shipwreck. Someone must have taken him to Devon — they said some people evaded capture from Captain Pierre's boat. Your baby must have gone away with one of your friends. Charlie was saved and Luis wrote a letter. I have the letter. He ... he asks after Charlie in it, but it's addressed to a tavern in Clovelly. They changed his name to Charles Oke. They stayed in Clovelly, and the letter from the Tolbooth — Luis' letter — found its way to them. He says those words in the letter. '*Fiat et Revirescit*'. I don't know what happened after that. I just know he was looked after, and he grew up and had his own family. *My* family.' I feel my eyes widen, and I flip my hand beneath Billy's so I can grip his convulsively. He grips it just as convulsively back. 'It makes sense now. I'm ...I'm related to him, to you, I think.' My head starts to spin and suddenly it all fits into place.

Charles Oke was born Charlie Ochoa. His parents were Mhairi and Luis. In the short time Luis spent at the Tolbooth, he'd manged to send a letter to Charlie's guardians at the tavern in Clovelly — knowing that was where they had arranged to send the baby if, as Mhairi said, 'the worst happened'. I can only imagine there was a network of Jacobites throughout the country — the friends that Mhairi spoke of — who helped transport baby Charlie to Devon, where they finally changed his identity to hide his origin and gave him a chance at a new life in an uncertain world. I could only imagine the pain of Charlie's parents as they wondered what had become of their baby — Luis awaiting his execution in an Edinburgh gaol, writing that one last letter, and Mhairi, separated from everyone and everything she knew and loved, finally coming to grief in the middle of the sea somewhere, when she was only trying to reach safety.

No wonder she had unfinished business.

This was the sort of unfinished business that tethered spirits to the earth — not my sort of unfinished business, not my wanderlust, or the idea of seeing what was over the next hill, or past the next river, or hiding away in the next village or town, just waiting to be discovered.

But I kind of understood that side of me now — good God, I was related to a so-called Spanish pirate; to a pair of eighteenth century rebels, more or less. To someone who was still searching for her home and her family after over 250 years . . .

To Mhairi Clouston and Luis Martinez Ochoa.

'Aye.' Mhairi looks straight at me. 'I said ye had his eyes, didn't I? Ma wee bairn. And Luis bloody Ochoa. Ma soulmate. Ma one true love.' She smiles faintly, and her shoulders relax a little. She nods across at the mortsafe. 'That's what it says there. Luis taught me to read. I know what it says, even though it's in thon funny language. It says, 'Not all of me will die'. It has to be true when you have a bairn, doesn't it? For ye live on through your bairn.'

She drifts off somewhere, her eyes softening as she apparently thinks of her true love; her dashing, heroic, piratical, rebel smuggler type, who gave his life to save hers and their baby's. I choke back my own sobs and bite my lip hard.

'Of course — ' she says, suddenly matter-of-fact ' — it dinnae mek it *ony* better that I'm stuck here. Bound here! By yon wee *felkyo*. What can we do about it, eh? What can we *do*?'

She looks at Billy expectantly, and I look at him expectantly, and he pales. 'Ummm,' he says. 'I might just have to make a phone call about that one.'

9

Billy

Lexie's recovered a bit from the shock. She seems to have taken it quite well, I think — the fact I see ghosts. Although, to be fair, when I mentioned that fact, it may well have been at the point where I thought she was about to run away or pass out, so it's possible she hasn't fully processed it. Anyway, she is watching me now, her eyes like saucers. 'Who's the *felkyo*?' she asks in a whisper. 'A witch, yeah? There's *really* a witch?' She looks a bit pale, and who can blame her really?

I swallow hard. 'Two. That we know of. Maybe three. Ha ha. Welcome to my illogical family.' I smile, my lips stretching across my teeth in what is probably another dreadful parody of the McCreadie Winning Smile.

'Who?' She looks stunned and dis-believing yet cautiously interested. Her gaze darts over to Mhairi and back again, and I reckon that if she sees and believes in the fact that Mhairi is there, and that I can see her and talk to her as well, then she might well believe that my family is not the most normal family in the world.

'Ummm. Nessa, for one. And Isabel, Clearly. She's the one responsible for all this. Something about a love spell that turned into a binding spell, and she bound the wrong sodding people. Or person.' I feel my cheeks burn and nod angrily over to Mhairi, who has a face like thunder and her lips compressed in a thin little line as she glares at me, awaiting resolution. 'And I have yet to be convinced that Maggie May is all sunshine and flowers. She's got Scott's genes, after all.'

'Scott? Your brother? But he's not a witch . . . warlock? Whatever? Is he?'

'No. Truth be told, we feel he has more to do with sodding fallen angels, and then there's Hugo.' I scroll through my phone angrily, picking out Nessa's number. 'Bloody Celtic legends abound in his sodding life. Then Alfie — ha! Who knows about Alfie? Who sodding knows? Nessa? Are you still pissed?' I bark out the words.

'William! Maybe just a little bit,' she says, giggling girlishly. If she was in front of me, I'd probably be tempted to throttle her, I really would.

'Well sober up, buttercup. I need advice.'

'William!' She sounds aghast. 'But I'm having *fun*.'

'And I'm not. Look, we're at the kirk-yard — '

'When you say 'we', who do you mean?'

'Lexie. And Me. And,' I close my eyes in despair, 'Mhairi.'

'Oh!' Nessa immediately perks up. 'All of you? Wow. Is Schubert there?'

'No. Schubert is with Maria and Hugo.'

'Oh! Yes. Yes, of course. So he said.'

I don't answer. Why would I answer that? Why would Nessa even *say* that? Lexie raises her eyebrows at me at the mention of her name. I shake my head and awkwardly wriggle my hand around so I can pat hers.

'So, there are the three of you. The unholy trinity. Interesting.'

'Nessa!'

'All right.' She sounds affronted, then her next words sound surprisingly sober. 'If Isa accidentally did a binding spell, and the three of you were there when she did it, then the three of you are bound. That means if Mhairi needs to go anywhere, you both have to take her. She maybe needs to settle her own ghosts, aye? Bury her own demons? Go somewhere to give her closure?'

There's a silence on the line as I process the info. 'Aye. Thank you, Nessa. I think I know what we need to do.'

'Good. I love you, Billy. Good luck.'

Half-reluctantly, I smile into the phone. 'Love you too, Nessa. Thanks again. Oh, and you might want to have a chat with Isabel — talk about consequences. That sort of thing.' Yes — *I handled that well, I think.*

'No problem. And Scott already

knows. She's grounded. No more Witchy Consultancy for a month. I felt it was my duty, even though I love her, to advise him of her Witchy Propensities. We can't have her misusing Her Gift.' There's those capitals again, and an ominous note in Nessa's voice. She's only ominous until the next sentence though, when she perks up. 'It's okay though, as Schubert is on his way over to comfort her.' She disconnects the call and I'm left with a disconnected *buzzzzzz* in my ear.

I wouldn't have liked to have been Scott when he delivered that news — I remember Scott's rages when we were kids. I'd imagine Isabel's would rival that with bells on. At least Schubert was on his way over to defuse it. That was something.

'I think I know what we need to do.' I direct the comment to Lexie and smile. This time the smile must be more genuine and not so vampiric or freaky, because her eyes widen momentarily and she smiles back at me, a little warily, but it's a smile, nonetheless.

'Cool. And your talent? It's just the . . . um . . . ghosts, yeah? If you've got witches and angels and living, breathing Celtic folklore people in your family, ghosts must be pretty . . . normal? Tame. Sort of?'

'Aye. It's pretty simple.' I flick a glance at Mhairi who, despite herself, looks a little bit interested in the answer as well. 'Like I said, I do indeed see dead people. Lots of them. And I talk to them.' I risk another smile. 'Why do you think I love this place so much? You get a great conversation out of almost anybody, at any time of the day or night, and they're always happy to see me.'

I wonder if I've shared too much but, thankfully, it appears that I haven't. Lexie looks startled for a minute, then bursts into wobbly laughter and shakes her head.

Then she leans into me again and closes her eyes . . .

And it's still pretty mind-blowing, I think, kissing a girl with a lip-ring.

It's something I'd definitely like to try

again and again and again . . .

Especially if that girl is Lexie Farrington.

It's just a bit difficult to do it properly
and really appreciate it when I'm tuning
out half of Edinburgh's restless spirits
who've all popped out of their tombs to
have a good look and cheer me on.

I'm not telling Lexie that one, though.
I think dealing with Mhairi is quite
enough for now.

Lexie

'Oooh. Hasn't it changed? Hasn't it
changed?'

Mhairi is so loud that I find it hard to
believe that people can't see her or hear
her.

We're at the kirkyard gates, Billy and
I hand in hand, and Mhairi peering
eagerly through the bars.

'Mhairi you must have seen all of this.'
Billy mutters the words tiredly. 'You
can't tell me that you've sat on that same

patch of grass for days. You followed me to the other gates last time I was here!'

'Aye. But look. *Look*!' She points at a bus on one of the nearby streets. 'Because *that* wisnae there *last* time I looked.'

'It's a bus. People travel in it. They come and go all the time. Good grief.' He shakes his head and looks at me despairingly. 'This is it. We have to try it.'

'It' is getting Mhairi from Greyfriars to the seashore at Leith. We think — or at least Billy thinks on the basis of speaking to Nessa — that the three of us can walk there together. Mhairi, he reckons, needs to visit the site of Luis' execution and come to terms with everything to help her move on to him in the afterlife. He also reckons that Mhairi is only bound in the kirkyard if the three of us are not together. If the three of us *are* together then we move a bit like a pack, and we can wander around Edinburgh to our hearts' content and hopefully take her where she needs to go.

'Try it, try it, try it . . . ' Mhairi begins to chant in that odd accent of hers, then grabs the railings and rattles them, looking up at Billy hopefully. 'Ye've nowt to lose. Try it, try it — '

'All *right*!' He takes a deep breath and steps outside of the cemetery. As we are holding hands, I have no choice but to do the same.

I look back at Mhairi, who suddenly appears to have cold feet and be hanging back. 'But . . . what if it's the wrong thing to do?' she asks a little bit pitifully.

'And what if it's not?' I'm still not entirely certain that this isn't all some odd dream, but, on the basis of Billy's hand feeling very warm and very real, I try to convince Mhairi that she has to try this.

Because if she doesn't, and she's stuck here forever mourning her lost love, then I'm going to feel pretty shit about not trying to convince her otherwise.

'I dinnae ken. It's weird. It's weird and it's witchcraft and I dinnae ken'

'The only thing that has anything to do with witchcraft is the fact that you're stuck here,' I say.

'But — but — but . . . witchcraft.' She turns and stomps back up the steps, then stomps back down them. 'It's nae right. That, that out there — it's no' ma world. It's no' right. Yon massive . . . things . . . on them big pathways. The noise! Oh my, the noise!' She plugs her ears with her fingers whilst staring at another bus rumbling past.

'It's the only way. You have to come with us.'

'No. No. No.'

'Mhairi — '

'Oooh, but it's different to the Islands. Tell you whit, I tell you whit, ye gan and get Luis and bring him here. Here. Right here.' She points to the ground she's standing on and bounces on the balls of her feet to drive it home.

'I don't think we could do that. I think the only way is for you to come with us,' says Billy. His mouth is looking decidedly more set now, and more angry. 'Binding spell, aye? So, you're bound to us. Luis isn't bound to anybody.'

'He is, he's bound to me. We swore it

at Odin's Stone. He's mine and I'm his and he can come here. Here.' She points again to the ground.

'I get that you're scared.' I try to reassure her. 'But it's not a big deal. You've got us.'

'No, no, no. No, I've changed ma mind. He can come here.' Again she jabs her finger earthwards. 'Here. I'm not goin' onywhare.'

And she folds her arms and pouts.

Billy

Mhairi is being 'difficult', as our mum used to say — and indeed still does say about Nessa at times.

I'm trying hard not to lose my temper as it's a weird situation for us all, but perhaps the only way to convince her is to try some reverse psychology. Reverse para-psychology, even.

'Okay.' I turn away from the gates. 'No worries. See you whenever, Miss Clouston.'

'Whit?' She unfolds her arms and looks stunned. She scuttles to the gate and stares up at me. 'Ye aint't leavin' me, are ye?'

'Aye. I am that. Come on, Lexie. Mhairi wants to stay here on her own with nobody to talk to.' I make as if to walk off. Lexie seems to immediately understand what I'm doing.

'Okay.' She shrugs her shoulders and starts to walk off with me.

'No! No! No! Come back. Come *back*, I tell ye!' My guess is that Mhairi is furious, but I'm determinedly not looking at her so I don't know for sure.

'Bye.' I keep walking off, and she swears a bit more and rattles the gates, demanding I return.

Then she swears in a very brilliant and inspired Nordic fashion — she really does have the mouth of a sailor — and there's one final massive metallic rattle, then suddenly there's an icy-cold edge to my body. I still refuse to look, although I'm certain that she's standing right next to me.

I don't have to look to feel the anger emanating from her spirit as I try to hide a smile.

'I'm here. I'm here. Now, take me to him before I regret ever trusting ye!' She sounds petulant, and I slyly cast my eye sideways and see her folding her arms again, then unfolding them and stomping purposefully along next to us. She doesn't even grumble when a bus rumbles past.

'I think we'll take the Water of Leith pathway,' I say to nobody in particular. 'It's a fair hike, but it'll take us straight to the seaside. And we need to get cracking before it gets too late.'

'I'm up for a healthy walk,' says Lexie, and I can tell she's joining in the game from the suppressed amusement in her voice.

'Oh, whit the hell. Me too,' Mhairi pipes up.

I nod, still without looking at her. 'Lovely afternoon for it. Let's try to enjoy it, eh?'

'Yes,' says Lexie. 'Let's.'

'Eejit,' mutters Mhairi. But I know she's going to come with us — and I pray that, however annoying and stubborn she is on the journey, that we can at least help her to get closure.

She's right, after all. Modern-day Edinburgh is no place for a Jacobite girl from the Orkneys.

Lexie

We've followed the Water of Leith pathway all along the river. Our journey has been interspersed with Mhairi's commentary and her occasional grumbling and her loudly sporadic shrieks of joy as she spots an interesting piece of scenery or a tree or a house, but, eventually, we reach our destination.

It's taken a good couple of hours, my feet are aching and it's getting on to evening, but we're now standing on a paved area called The Shore, looking across to where Billy suggests the Sands of Leith might have been — at the east end of the harbour.

Well, we're as close as we can probably get; the shoreline will have definitely altered somewhat. I don't think we'll be able to get over to the 'proper' Sands area, which is maybe a good thing as I notice Billy is already looking a bit discomfited — I imagine there are quite a few restless spirits hanging around there, ready to pop out and go 'Hello!'

There's not much to look at nowadays over where The Sands were to be honest, except some concrete and some buildings and some big old ships and an old Martello tower, which was probably built in the war; it's all a bit grim, really. I don't know what I expected, but I was hoping for a little more sand and some pretty beachy views; something a bit more romantic.

I feel a bit bad for Mhairi, as she appears next to me and grumbles again. 'I appreciate the thought, I do, but I cannae see how this horrid place is anywhere near where ma Luis will be. I mean — '

She suddenly stops speaking and

points a shaking finger at a spot on the harbour, where there's one of those bollard things that they tie boats up to. 'Oh my. Oh my. Oh *my* . . .'

Then there's like a *whoosh* and a veritable whirlwind whips up out of nowhere, blowing my hair into my face and into my open mouth, as I'm poised to speak.

And then she's gone. She's just disappeared into thin air.

'Billy?' I spit the hair out of my mouth and ask the question hesitantly, as he's staring at the bollard as well.

'I saw him. I saw him — Luis. He was there. Sitting on that thing looking really miserable . . . ' His voice trails off and he looks at me. 'Did *you* see him?'

I peer back at the bollard, ready to shake my head, because really, what's the chances of me seeing *two* ghosts in one day? I've literally only been a sort-of believer for a few hours and it still feels a bit odd. But I couldn't deny that I saw and heard Mhairi at all, and I trust Billy. I really do trust him.

So, of course it's real. Of *course* it is.

I blink and re-focus on the bollard . . .

And actually, there's a whisper of a shadow there; the shape of a man, sitting on the bollard, his chin in his hands. Another figure appears next to him, a rainbow whirlwind with bright, golden shafts of light penetrating it and a tartan haze surrounding it. I gasp. It has to be her — it *has* to be Mhairi, rushing towards Luis, who must be the lost-looking man sitting on the bollard. Mhairi is certainly not with us any more anyway; the energy she was fizzing with has just vanished and the air around me feels . . . different.

I glance up at Billy in confusion, and he's still looking at me. Our eyes lock and I understand what the new energy is — it's us. It's just *us*. It's like a promise of something to come, like we're just on the verge of something. I feel a little dizzy, and there's a rushing in my ears that echoes the sound of the sea rushing into the harbour close by.

'*Do* you see them?' His brows furrow and he points at the bollard again, but he's not even *looking* over at where he's pointing.

He's looking at me.

And I'm looking at him.

And there's nothing else I can focus on.

'Yes.' My voice is small and trembly. 'I can see them. Has the spell been broken then? The binding spell? Does it mean there's only . . . us?'

'Yes. I think it does mean that. She doesn't need to be with us any more. She's found her true love again, and you can probably bet that she won't be thinking about us at *all*.'

I tear my gaze away from him, forcing myself not to look into those eyes or notice the way the gentle sea-breeze lifts his hair around his face. I peer at the bollard and nothing looks different at all. Not a thing. I squint, wondering if I might see a vague outline of her, of them both, even. A bit of shimmery . . . something. I strain my ears to try and catch a faint murmur of Mhairi's odd, musical voice. But there's nothing.

'She's gone. She's just . . . not there.' I shake my head, feeling a weird mix of sad, miffed and happy. Sad and miffed that she's just buggered off without a word, but happy that she's found Luis after all these years, and that we've helped her.

It's a lovely feeling, actually.

'She *is* there.. They're *both* there — but don't look now, Lexie. You *really* don't want to be seeing what they're getting up to. But I think it's more important, somehow, that *we* are here. And maybe that we're still . . . sort of . . . bound? Or something?'

Billy's cheeks colour, and I stand on tiptoe and press my lips against his briefly. 'I don't mind that. Do you?'

He shakes his head, and a smile grows as he does so. Then he lowers his face down towards me. His voice is soft but full of promise, and my stomach does that wibbly thing again. 'I don't mind in the slightest.'

'There's a hotel right here,' I hear myself saying.

'It's been a long day.'

206

'It has.'

'I could do with a nap.'

'Me too.'

'It's getting quite late. Sunset practically.'

Then we grin at each other and start to laugh, and he pulls me even closer and together we turn to walk away from the harbour, away from the ocean and away from Mhairi, Luis and their somewhat grisly past.

The future, I think, looks pretty awesome from where I'm standing — and I think Billy and I are kind of bound to agree on that one . . .

10

A few weeks later

Billy

We've borrowed Nessa's camper van and parked it up on the roadside of the B9055, north east of Stromness on Orkney, and we're heading across the grass to the Standing Stones of Stenness. In this circle is the imposing Odin Stone — a big grey column with a hole in it.

It's the stone that Mhairi said she'd visited with Luis, where they swore their love to one another.

'Mow wow.'

Of course, it isn't a show without Punch, and Schubert had to come as well, but he hasn't been bad company. He curled up in his cat carrier with Catnip and snored all the way here. Borrowing Winnie Bago, Nessa's yellow camper van, was a trade-off. She said we could, so long as I fixed a weird rattle under the bonnet and Schubert came with us for a little holiday.

I can't escape that bloody cat. But Lexie and I, we're making the best of it and having a long weekend, involving a trip around the Islands. We were both desperate to come here. Lexie said she fancied a bit more travelling, and then wondered out loud if she needed to get it out of her system. Then she bit her lip and frowned a great deal.

She reminded me a lot of Mhairi.

Anyway, we both wanted to see where Mhairi's story began — where it all started. So we just decided to go for it.

'It's beautiful up here, isn't it?' I'm staring out at the scenery, taking in the sea just across from us and the narrow stretch of road that joins two bits of land together across that very same sea. 'You can really feel what it would have been like here. I suspect it hasn't changed that much. Apart from the main road being there, of course.' I look down at Lexie and can't help smiling. 'I can see how a local girl would have been swept away by a dashing piratical hero with an exotic accent.'

'Maybe not even a local girl.' Lexie smiles up at me and she's even more beautiful to look at than the scenery. 'Maybe a girl from very far away might be swept away by one, too. And there's a lot to be said for a Scottish accent, you know?'

'Do you reckon?'

'I reckon. But I might not be too far away at all if I get this job.'

Lexie has discovered there's a job going at the National Records of Scotland in Edinburgh. She said that she thought, perhaps, it was time for her to move on again. A bit further north, she said, a bit more towards, or even *into* Scotland, she said. Perhaps even *Edinburgh*, she said. Then she blushed a bit and chewed her lip again, but I kissed her and she was fine after that. We agreed we'd have a look at her application form together one evening as the sun doesn't set until well into the night here. Lexie said she thought there was something desperately romantic about sitting out-side, looking at the mountains and the water and breathing in the pure north-ern air.

I can't disagree with her.

I must confess, before she spotted the job, I said I was happy to go down south to do my teaching degree. However, it seemed that she didn't want that.

'I want to come back up here,' she said. 'To come home to Scotland ... where I feel my heart might *properly*, finally, belong.'

I told her I would feel I was at home then as well, which was, as she said, 'bonkers, because you already live here, you dafty.'

But strangely, I knew exactly what she meant — which was equally bonkers.

Lexie

Billy is just looking down at me and smil-ing and smiling, and I know he's thinking the same things I am. I can't actually wait until I'm up here properly. I think I'll get that job, I really do. And funnily enough, once I get it, I've the feeling I'll stay put for quite some time.

I'll stay put for as long as Billy stays put, most definitely. I mean, who knows what the future might hold for two wanderers like us? But I know Billy McCreadie, pirate extraordinaire, will be in my future whatever I do. I absolutely know it.

'Come on, Lexie.' Billy interrupts my thoughts and nods across to the Odin Stone in the middle of the circle. 'Let's have a closer look. Do you know much about the legends attached to this thing?'

'No. Enlighten me, please.' There's amusement in my voice and I know it.

'With pleasure.' There's a matching amusement in his. 'There was a custom in the 1700s, probably from even earlier, where people would all get together at what they called the Kirk of Stainhouse on the first day of every new year, and they'd basically party for four or five days at the Kirk. It gave them all a chance to meet other people, and they reckon a few couples got married every year from that party.'

'Gives a whole new meaning to celebrating Hogmanay, doesn't it?'

'Absolutely. But here. Read this.' He pulls out something from his pocket; it looks like a printout of some kind. 'This was written by Reverend George Low, the minister of Birsay and Harray, in 1774. I can't use any better words myself to describe Mhairi's world.'

'Intriguing.' I unfold it, and I smile as I read it.

The parties agreed stole from the rest of their companions, and went to the Temple of the Moon, where the woman, in presence of the man, fell down on her knees and prayed the god Wodden (for such was the name of the god they addressed upon this occasion) that he would enable her to perform all the promises and obligations she had and was to make to the young man present, after which they both went to the Temple of the Sun, where the man prayed in like manner before the woman, then they repaired from this to the stone, known as Wodden's or Odin's

Stone, and the man being on one side and the woman on the other, they took hold of each other's right hand through the hole, and there swore to be constant and faithful to each other. This ceremony was held so very sacred in those times that the person who dared to break the engagement made here was counted infamous, and excluded all society.

'How wonderful.' I can't stop smiling. 'Do you think this is what Mhairi and Luis did?' I walk up to the stone and peer through the hole to the other side—

'Hello! Hello, hello, *hello*! How nice to see ye, how very, very *nice*!'

A pale, pretty face is grinning at me through the gap.

'Mhairi!' My heart lurches and I stare back at her, shocked. 'Is it you? Really? Or what . . . am I *really* bonkers?'

'Mow wow!' Schubert suddenly yowls in excitement and rushes over to the stone — he's been waddling around the edge of the circle for a little while, and I wondered if he was looking for a good place to have a wee, but he's obviously

214

decided this is more important. 'Mow wow!'

'And hallo to ye too, ye wee beastie! I've missed ye, I have.' Mhairi's face disappears south as she apparently kneels down to fuss Schubert.

'Billy?' I step away from the stone, wondering if I'm actually dreaming — if I've genuinely fallen asleep or if the magic of this ancient place has somehow worked its way into my bones. I turn around to speak to him, but there's another dark-haired, piratical type standing there . . .

Oh my God. He is absolutely gorgeous. Absolutely drop-dead gorgeous. He looks much better close up than he did sitting on that bollard.

'Señorita Alexandrina.' He bows and I stare at him, my jaw dropping before I can make myself look less vacant. 'How can I thank you for bringing her back to me?'

His voice is, as I might have guessed, heavily accented with Spanish, and his eyes are — well — his eyes are exactly like mine. It's a weird, weird feeling.

'Ummm . . . errrr . . .' I can't quite formulate a response.

Luis — for this has to be him — smiles and bows again, his eyes twinkling. 'You do not have to answer right now. But believe it when I say that I am undyingly grateful to you.' He sounds a bit like Antonio Banderas. 'I see you've inherited our son's good looks. It is a pleasure to meet you at last, Alexandrina.' He grins mischievously.

'Ummm . . . errrr . . . you too . . . Luis.' If feels wrong to be calling him Great Great whatever Grandfather. Because then isn't Mhairi my . . . Great Great whatever Granny? It just all feels too weird.

Mind blowing.

'Ah. Awesome.' This time it's Billy who speaks. He appears from around the other side of the stone, Schubert waddling excitedly at his feet, occasionally trying to reach up and paw him for some reason — probably because he's fed up of actually waddling and wants to be picked up.

Mhairi is bouncing around beside them. She looks gorgeous herself; she's cleaned up a treat. Her long, blonde, curly hair appears washed and combed, and her tartan skirt is all nice and swishy and fresh-looking. Her bodice is a bit more decent as well. 'Lexie, Mhairi — I see you've met again then. It's nice to see you too, Luis. Properly, that is.' Billy gives him a little respectful bow. 'Mhairi told us all about you. I saw you — briefly — at Leith.'

'Ahhh, now *that* I wish to forget.' He flaps his hand elegantly around. 'And I can do that by being here. With my lover.'

'I'm so happy I've ceased the dripping thing!' pipes up Mhairi and claps her hands together in delight.

Luis looks down at her fondly. 'I love you if you drip or not, my darling.'

He pronounces it 'dreep'.

Billy glances around. 'You're not the only ones who've come back,' he says. 'Seems like the clan is out to welcome you. You needn't have worried.'

I look around as well, my stomach

lurching ever so slightly. I can't see any-body or anything apart from Mhairi and Luis, who are standing together now, hand in hand. But, all of a sudden, there's an even stranger strange feeling about the place. I shiver.

'Enjoy it. Enjoy coming home.' Billy seems unfazed and happy to have seen it all. He smiles at them. 'We'll leave you to it.'

He reaches his hand out for mine, but I shake my head. 'No.'

'Mow wow.' Schubert nods approv-ingly like he knows what I'm going to suggest.

'No?' Billy looks confused and his arm flails around, lost. 'I thought . . .'

'You probably thought right,' I tell him. 'But we need to do it properly. Come on.' I look at the Odin Stone and take a deep breath. I put my right hand through the hole and wiggle my fingers. 'I can't promise you five solid days of partying in my company, but will you do this with me?'

Realisation dawns and Billy laughs

out loud, looking a little bit relieved. 'Aye. Aye, I will.' He strides around to the other side of the stone and grabs my right hand with his right one.

His fingers are warm in mine, and I think we both feel the strange energy that wraps around us. It's like warmth and excitement and hope and magic, all rolled into one.

'Odin has given us his blessing,' Billy says quietly.

'I think he has.'

'My problem is now, that I want to kiss you, really badly, and to do that I'll have to leave go of your hand and come around there to see you...' Then he raises my hand to his lips and presses them against it. 'But I don't want to leave go, I really don't.'

'Me neither.'

'Mow wow.' Schubert, it seems, still agrees.

Then there's that weird whirlwind again, and faint laughter is brought in on it, along with the sea-salt tang of the ocean. I realise Mhairi and Luis are

219

nowhere to be seen, but I get an overwhelming sense of joy and acceptance sweeping around that stone circle. I know they'll soon be back where they're supposed to be, and I doubt I'll ever see either of them again after today.

I don't think I want to see *any* more ghosts after today, to be fair — but, if I'm bound to Billy McCreadie, who knows what will happen?

Then Billy's voice interrupts my thoughts. 'I'll have to do it, I think. Leave go of your hand, that is. For now.'

'For now.' My hair whips up in the wind, then settles again. It's all gone quiet and there's that tingly shift in the energy again.

'But not forever. I'm not leaving go forever.' Billy's eyes drill into me and my legs suddenly feel like jelly.

'Not forever.'

'Mow wow.' And it seems that Schubert really *does* agree, and he waddles off nicely, his tail in the air, heading towards what I can only assume is Mhairi, as he starts prancing around thin air and pawing at where her skirt would be.

There's a brief moment where he's lifted from the ground and cradled in someone's invisible arms, then I turn away and close my eyes against a fat black cat hovering in mid-air — and the gentle pressure of Billy's hand holding my hand disappears, and a moment later I feel his lips on mine again, and it's wonderful.

I know it's exactly where I'm meant to be.

And then he's holding my hand again — both hands, actually — and I know we'll never let go of one another; not really. Not ever.

Because, you see, I'm Home.

We do hope that you have enjoyed
reading this large print book.

Did you know that all of our titles
are available for purchase?

We publish a wide range of high
quality large print books including:
Romances, Mysteries, Classics
General Fiction
Non Fiction and Westerns

Special interest titles available in
large print are:
The Little Oxford Dictionary
Music Book, Song Book
Hymn Book, Service Book

Also available from us courtesy of
Oxford University Press:
Young Readers' Dictionary
(large print edition)
Young Readers' Thesaurus
(large print edition)

For further information or a free
brochure, please contact us at:
Ulverscroft Large Print Books Ltd.,
The Green, Bradgate Road, Anstey,
Leicester, LE7 7FU, England.
Tel: (00 44) **0116 236 4325**
Fax: (00 44) **0116 234 0205**

Other titles in the
Linford Romance Library:

LOVE IN LAVENDER LANE

Jill Barry

Fiona exchanges her quiet suburban world for 1970s London when she inherits her great-aunt's marriage bureau near Marble Arch. But she has never been truly in love, so it's going to be a challenge arranging perfect pairings for her starry-eyed clients . . . While Fiona's busy interviewing and arranging introductions, how will she ever find time to make her own dream come true? And could it be that she and her most difficult client to match are actually meant for one another?

THE LOVE TREE

Patricia Keyson

When Lily arrives at The Limes to work as a maid for two sisters, Eta and Mabel, little does she know she will instantly fall in love with their handsome lodger, Samuel. When Cecil Potts visits the sisters' beer house and shop, a tale of murder, death and deceit unravels. Will Lily and Samuel ever step out from Cecil's dark shadow to find happiness under the love tree?

ANNIE'S CASTLE BY THE SEA

Christina Garbutt

After a lifetime of putting her daughter first, widowed Annie travels to the beautiful Italian island of Vescovina for a summer. Annie's soon swept up in the magic of the place, but when the town is under threat by developers it's up to Annie and her gorgeous new friend, Giovanni, to save it. But as pressure begins to mount, is it really the town that needs saving — or Annie's heart?

GREEN SKIES AT NIGHT

Alan C. Williams

When a wide-ranging Green Skies weather phenomenon threatens the people of Tulsa, Oklahoma with destruction, it's up to meteorologist Amber Devane to warn them. The trouble is, the local media don't believe her predictions. She must put aside her recovery from an operation to save her family and her county. Aided by school-friend Ryan, a native American astronomer, the two of them must fight the tumultuous weather and prejudices as well as struggle with their own whirlwind budding romance . . .

PENNYWISE

Ewan Smith

Penny can't wait to go on the holiday of a lifetime with her best friend, Angela. But then comes some terrible news: her father has had a heart-attack. Now she will have to spend the summer looking after her parents' little seaside shop instead. That wouldn't be so bad but the neighbouring LoPrice supermarket has its eyes on the property. And Penny isn't sure what to make of the assistant manager, Graham Fraser. He's young, good-looking — and very ambitious.